DATE DUE

MAY 13 69			
MAY 20 69			
NOV 21 69			
DEC 5 69			
OCT 23 70			
NOV 12 70			
NOV 30 70			
DEC 7			
DEC 12 72			

Heuman, William
Left end Luisetti

"Gino Luisetti is slowly accepted by his teammates — all but Whip Grogan, that is. The development of understanding and responsibility among the team members, with their answer to some problems of delinquency, give depth to the story."

— Library Journal

B 8-329

left end Luisetti

left end Luisetti

by

WILLIAM HEUMAN

STECK-VAUGHN COMPANY
PUBLISHERS • AUSTIN, TEXAS

LIBRARY OF CONGRESS
CATALOG CARD NUMBER 58-10487

. . . for JANET

ONE

When the bell rang, ending the English 2 class, Gino Luisetti picked up his books and followed the crowd out into the hall. Other rooms along the corridor of the big City High were emptying also, and the corridor was soon jammed with high-school students moving in both directions to new classes.

Many of them walked in groups, laughing, joking, but Gino walked alone, his books tight under his arm, staring straight ahead of him. He was a fairly tall boy for fourteen, and a sophomore at City High. His eyes were dark brown to go with his straight black hair, high cheek bones, and olive complexion.

"Hey, Gino," a boy called behind him. "Hey, *Italiano.*"

Gino slowed down, his tense face relaxing a little, recognizing the voice. If someone else had made reference to his nationality, he would have

1

resented it, and that invisible wall would have come up between himself and the other boy, but with little Benny Irvine it was different. Benny was good humor, personified. *Italiano*, with him, was a mark of affection.

"What do you think of that English composition?" Benny chuckled. "We gotta write on, 'What We Like Best about City High.' How do you like that, Gino?"

Gino just shrugged, and there was cold humor in his brown eyes. What did he like best about City High? *Nothing,* he thought bitterly. *Nothing at all.*

"How about McCarthy?" Benny grinned. "How about that Wayne McCarthy? I think I'll write about McCarthy. That'll kill the class."

They were heading down to the gymnasium now for the Physical Training period, P.T. 2. Wayne McCarthy—the hated Mr. McCarthy—the gym teacher, was in charge of P.T. 2.

"He's in charge of jayvee football this year," Benny was saying as he hurried along, trying to match Gino's long stride down the corridor. "I almost decided not to try out."

Gino looked down at the short, stubby boy with the brown hair and the large nose. Benny Irvine was not a handsome boy. His nose was too large, and his mouth was too large, but he had good eyes, quiet brown eyes. When you looked at his eyes, you forgot about his face.

"You going out for jayvee?" Gino asked, surprised.

"Sure," Benny nodded. "First practice tomorrow afternoon."

"You're too little," Gino pointed out. "They'll kill you."

"When you're built low," Benny chuckled, "you don't have to fall so far. I'm going out for the line —maybe guard."

"They'll walk all over you," Gino said.

"So let 'em walk," Benny laughed. "Next year, or the year after, when I've put on more weight, I'll walk on them. So what?"

They went down the stairs at the far end of the corridor, and when they reached the main floor, they turned left and entered the big gymnasium, turning in at the first door to the locker room.

"You going out for the team?" Benny wanted to know.

"No," Gino said. He didn't care for the tough, hard-faced, pugnacious Wayne McCarthy, gym teacher and jayvee coach. It was enough that he had to take Physical Training under McCarthy. He didn't want to see any more of him after the regular school session.

"You could make it," Benny said thoughtfully.

3

"You can run like a deer, Gino, and you've played a lot of football in the street."

"Not the same as on a football field," Gino pointed out. "We never played real tackle, only touch tackle."

They moved down between the rows of green-painted iron lockers until they came to their own, far down the line. There were combination locks on the lockers, and both boys turned the dials, mechanically, until they were able to open the doors.

"I never played real tackle, either," Benny observed. "You don't play tackle on pavement, but if you can run, and catch a football, and throw it, that's all you need to know. The rest you learn when you're on the squad."

"Not me," Gino said.

The locker room was jammed with boys who were taking P.T. 2 now. Locker doors banged open and closed. There was a lot of talk as they changed into gym shoes, and threw their street shoes into the lockers, along with books and jackets.

Benny Irvine said carefully, "You know Whip Grogan's going out for the team."

Gino shrugged but said nothing. Even if McCarthy hadn't been junior-varsity football coach, the fact that Whip Grogan was going out for the team would have been sufficient to keep Gino away from the field. Grogan was a neighborhood boy,

4

like Benny Irvine, but unlike Benny, a boy whom he hated.

The tough, confident, aggressive Grogan had always been top man in those football games in the street. He would make the jayvee team easily, and he would star on it, because he was good and because he knew he was good. This confidence buoyed him up, making him better than boys who were his equal or even superior to him in ability.

Gino wondered, enviously, how it felt to be like that, to walk down the street, and to know that you're as good or better than anybody else. Even as a very small boy it had not been that way with him—ever since he'd learned what his father did for a living in the city, and the boys on the block had started to jeer at him about it.

Benny was saying, "Grogan will go out for quarterback. He figures he'll make the varsity next year for sure."

"Let him," Gino said shortly.

Whip Grogan was about due now. He had a locker along the same bench where they were, but Grogan invariably came in late, taking his time, strolling leisurely out on the gym floor, his sneakers still untied. At that moment the buzzer would sound and they would get in line for calisthenics. Grogan never worried.

Some of the boys in the locker room had started to boo now, very softly at first, but it was beginning to pick up, and this was something every Wayne McCarthy P.T. class did. They booed McCarthy from the locker room where he couldn't see them because they disliked him, but it was a cowardly thing to do, and Gino never took part in it.

A boy swung around the corner of the locker, booing loudly, insolently, and encouraging the others. This was Whip Grogan, as tall as Gino but a little heavier in the shoulders. He was a red-haired boy with a lean, hard face and tough blue eyes.

"Boo!" Whip said. "Boo, McCarthy!"

He sat down in front of his small locker, fiddled with the combination lock all the while that he booed, and then yanked it open, banging the door against the next locker.

Gino sat about six feet away from him, putting on his sneakers, tightening the laces, waiting for Whip's remark, and knowing that it would come.

For the moment Whip was too busy booing the disliked Wayne McCarthy, but after awhile as he was kicking off his leather shoes he glanced over and started to sniff audibly. That was the way it always began—the sniffing, and the broad, sly grin.

"Smells like a sewer around here," Whip said.

Gino's olive-complexioned face turned a dull red, but he didn't look up.

6

"You down there yourself this morning, Gino?" Whip chuckled. "You down in the sewer with your old man?"

Still Gino didn't say anything. He knew that he didn't have an odor but that his father did, and any man would who spent all of his working hours under the ground in the city's huge sewer system.

Guiseppe Luisetti was a sewer maintenance man, and he knew every foot of the miles and miles of sewer lines. In the morning he went down into the sewers, and he didn't come out until late afternoon when his stint was done, and it was understandable that he would smell like it.

Arriving from Italy, thirty years before, the father had gotten this job with the city sanitation department. It was a good job, and it was the only kind of work he could get. After awhile a man could get used to the smell.

Whip said, "They shouldn't allow a smell like that in a place like this. Boo, McCarthy."

Benny Irvine said softly, "Let him talk, Gino."

"Hey, Benny," Whip called down along the bench. "I said to boo McCarthy."

"Okay," Benny nodded.

"Go ahead," Whip ordered.

"Boo, McCarthy," Benny said. He hadn't been booing before like a good many of the other boys, and he said it now in a soft voice.

"Can't hear you," Whip told him, and Benny booed slightly louder. "How about you, Gino?" Whip said.

"Never mind," Gino told him.

"You're not booing?"

"No," Gino said, and he sat up, looking straight at Whip.

"You like McCarthy?" Whip asked him.

"That's my business," Gino said. He wasn't afraid of Whip and never had been even though years before when they were both nine or ten years old, Whip had beaten him in a fight. Sooner or later they would have to fight again.

Benny Irvine said, "Come on, Gino. We have to run."

The buzzer was due to ring shortly, which meant that every boy had to be on the gym floor, and moving toward his position in the calisthenics class.

Whip just looked at Gino but said no more as Gino finished tying his shoelaces and started to follow Benny down toward the door leading out on the gym floor.

"Let him talk," Benny urged. "Words don't hurt, Gino."

"I don't like it," Gino scowled.

"He talks to me, too," Benny grinned. "He thinks he's pushing me around, but he's not. I'm laughing at him, inside. I think he knows that, too."

8

"With you it's different," Gino told him. "You're small. He'd never fight you."

"Just let him talk," Benny said. "What can he say? Just words."

Wayne McCarthy was striding out from the office now, moving toward the high platform from which he directed the exercises. He was a big man, solid shoulders, athletic, with a protruding jaw and a pugnacious face.

He had the reputation in the gym of working his classes harder than any of the other gym teachers. There were more knee-bends, more arm-lifts, more touching of the toes with the fingers, but it wasn't the work which made him unpopular; it was his attitude. He stood up on the high platform with that tough, uncompromising smile on his face, and he would order twenty or thirty knee-bends, leaving some of the heavier, less athletic boys staggering when they finished.

When the class was dismissed, then, in the locker room, the booing would begin.

Wayne McCarthy passed by Gino as he stood with Benny Irvine, and as he was going up the steps to the platform, the buzzer rang in the locker room. The tardy boys ran out through the doors, trotting to their positions on the floor.

There were a dozen lines of them—twelve boys

in a line, with about four feet separating each one so that there was room for the calisthenics.

Whip Grogan came out of the locker room last, trotting leisurely to his position, and he still wasn't there when the whistle blew from the platform.

Mr. McCarthy blew two short blasts on his whistle, and when Whip sheepishly turned around, the gym teacher pointed toward the office.

There were grins from the other boys in line as Whip slouched down toward the glass-enclosed office to have another 'tactic' mark registered against his name. Six tactics could flunk one in P.T., and so far as Gino knew Whip had three, and they had only been in school two weeks.

Benny Irvine grinned across at Gino in the next line as Whip went to the office for his tactic mark. Wayne McCarthy gave out at least five times as many tactic marks as the other gym teachers, and this was another reason for the booing. McCarthy's big finger would point at a boy, and then at the office door, and that was it. He gave out the tactics for not trying to do a particular exercise, for doing it slovenly, for missing a count—for almost anything —but Gino had to admit that his gym class was probably the finest in the school.

Mr. McCarthy had an announcement to make before he started calisthenics, and it concerned jay-vee football. He was asking for candidates for the junior varsity squad to turn out tomorrow afternoon at three-thirty on the school field.

Gino saw his tough blue eyes going over the long lines of boys in front of him, lingering particularly on the bigger boys in the rear of the lines. These were the candidates he wanted for his jayvee squad, and he was speaking especially to them.

"If you want to play varsity football at City High," Wayne McCarthy was saying, "you'd better begin with the jayvee squad. Any boy fourteen or over is invited to try out for the squad. We have a four-game schedule this year, and it's tough."

Whip had the demerit mark registered against his name in the book, and he came back to his position. Calisthenics got under way, and as usual Mr. McCarthy drilled them unmercifully.

When the session was over a few minutes before the bell rang, and the boys were in the locker room changing their shoes, the booing was louder than Gino had ever heard it.

He wondered what Mr. McCarthy thought of this booing. He probably could have stopped it if he had wanted to by sending a flying squadron of upperclass boys into the locker room to grab the chief offenders, but he did nothing. His P.T. class was no tougher than before. He gave out no more tactic marks than he had given out in the beginning. Gino had his respect for the man because of this.

Wayne McCarthy was hard, but he was not small and mean.

After P.T. there was one more class in Biology, and then Gino was finished for the day. Benny had Biology 2 with him, also, and they left the class together at about three o'clock, going out the west door of the big four-story, red brick building.

City High was one of the old schools, no particular style to it, a square block of a building, with the athletic field at the rear surrounded by a fifteen-foot high wire fence. There was a football field, and a soccer field, side by side. The soccer squad was not too big, and ordinarily the players were shifted elsewhere, and the jayvee football squad worked out on the soccer field.

Benny walked with Gino across the football field, which was empty as yet, none of the varsity players having come out. They usually left the grounds through the exit gate beyond the football field, walking the six blocks along the west side of the city to their homes.

As they approached the big open gate, they saw a boy standing there, his books on the concrete base of the gate. He was facing them, leaning back against the gate post, a cold grin on his face.

The boy wore a faded brown sweater, which was familiar, and he was hatless. His rust-colored hair caught the gleam of the late September sunshine, and the breeze ruffled it slightly.

Benny Irvine said slowly, "Looks like Whip Grogan is waiting for somebody, Gino."

Gino said nothing. He walked on slowly, deliberately, but with his heart beginning to pound a little. He was not afraid of Whip; he wasn't afraid of anybody, but he didn't like this.

TWO

Whip said when they came up, "You boys were kind of fresh in the locker room this afternoon."

"Why should we get fresh, Whip?" Benny grinned. "We like you."

"I don't believe it," Whip smiled. "How about it, Gino?"

"How about what?" Gino countered.

"You tip off Mr. McCarthy that I was booing him in the locker room?"

Gino stared at the red-headed boy. "I'd never do that," he said.

Benny said, open-mouthed, "Somebody told McCarthy that, Whip? What'd he do?"

"Not a thing," Whip scowled, "but I don't like it that somebody ratted on me." He was still staring at Gino. "How about it, Ginzo?"

That was always one of his pet names for Gino, and Gino hated it.

"I told you," Gino snapped, "I didn't do it."

"You could have," Whip smiled. "Anybody crawls out of a sewer hole—" He stopped because Gino was putting his books down on the concrete shelf. "Don't tell me," Whip murmured, his blue eyes narrowing.

"You want trouble," Gino told him thickly. "You've been asking for it, Whip."

Benny said quickly, "You'll get in trouble on the school grounds. Let's forget the whole thing."

"What'll he do," Whip smiled, "tell Mr. McCarthy there was a fight on the grounds?"

Gino squared off, his fists tight. He didn't talk now because he knew he couldn't keep his voice steady, and he didn't want Whip Grogan to laugh at him.

Whip started to advance on him, but he hadn't taken more than three steps before Benny hissed, "Here comes Mr. McCarthy."

Gino turned his head quickly to see Wayne Mc-Carthy striding toward them from the direction of one of the side doors of the school. Mr. McCarthy was wearing a pair of khaki pants and a gray sweat shirt. He was hatless.

"Let's get out," Benny whispered.

"I'm not runnin'," Whip said, and he sat down on the concrete shelf, waiting for Mr. McCarthy to come up.

Gino picked up his books, not certain what to do. He wasn't running away either. Mr. McCarthy had undoubtedly seen them from the building and knew what they were up to. He was coming over to reprimand them, and they had to wait until he arrived.

Wayne McCarthy's pale blue eyes were expressionless when he came up. He said simply, "Was that a fist fight getting under way?"

Whip said, "Yes."

Mr. McCarthy looked from one boy to the other, and then at little Benny sitting near the gate. He said, "You want to tell me what it was all about, or isn't it any of my business?"

"Our business," Whip said easily. "We would have settled it."

McCarthy frowned and shook his head. "You don't settle much with your fists," he said. "You only think you do. What are your names?"

They told him, and he said, "Both of you coming out for jayvee football?"

"I am," Whip said, but Gino shook his head.

McCarthy glanced at Gino curiously. "You have the build for it," he said. "You've probably played some in the street. Is that right?"

Gino nodded.

"But you don't want to play for City High?"

Gino shrugged. "I'm not much good at it," he

said sheepishly. "I—I go home in the afternoons."

Benny said suddenly, "Why don't you come out for the team, Gino?"

Gino glanced at Whip, seeing the small, derisive smile on his face, and it angered him.

"I'd try it if I were you," Wayne McCarthy said, and he was smiling a little now. Gino suddenly discovered that he was not the hard, ruthless taskmaster the boys thought he was. When he smiled, he looked different, not at all like Wayne McCarthy.

"I—I'll see," Gino mumbled.

"Three-thirty tomorrow afternoon," Mr. McCarthy told him. "I'll see both of you."

"Me, too," Benny said suddenly. "I'm trying out for the line."

Mr. McCarthy looked at him, and nodded. "Good," he said simply, and he walked away.

When the gym teacher was out of hearing, Whip said, "Why didn't you tell him right off that you didn't want to play?"

"I told him I'd think about it," Gino scowled.

"You might get bounced around a little on that field," Whip told him. "Maybe that's why you don't want to come out."

"If I wanted to play, I'd play," Gino flared.

"Prove it," Whip grinned, and he walked off, his books under his arm.

Benny Irvine said, "Well, that's that."

As they walked down the street together, passing long rows of brick tenement houses, and push carts in the streets, Gino thought about the talk with Wayne McCarthy, and Whip's remarks.

He had nothing to do in the afternoons. Usually, he did whatever homework he had to do, and he might run an errand or two for his mother, but there wasn't much of anything else. With his friends like Benny going out for football, there wouldn't be anybody around the block in the afternoons.

Benny's father had a tailor and dry-cleaning shop a few doors from Gino's house, and when Benny turned in at the shop, Gino went on down to his own house, walking up the three flights of stairs to the four-room apartment.

His mother was waiting for him when he came in.

"Gino," she beamed. *"Bambino."*

"No more baby," Gino scowled. "I'm grown up, Mom."

He sat down at the kitchen table, putting his books in front of him. He stared out the window and down at the drab back yard which separated this house from the one on the next street.

His mother said in Italian, "You are worried, Gino. What is it?"

Gino shrugged. He was the only child, and his parents had always been affectionate with him.

They'd given him the best that they were able, all the time.

"They want me to play football," he said, speaking in Italian.

"You do not want to play?" she asked.

Gino frowned. "I'm not sure," he said. He'd been sure, before, but since Whip had goaded him and taunted him, he'd been thinking about it. He had liked playing football in the streets, but playing for City High was something else. He didn't like the school; he didn't feel that he was part of it. It was a place where he went to learn things, but that was all. He was glad to get away from it when his last class was over. It wasn't that anybody had ever hurt him at City High, but it was a big school with several thousand students, and no one had ever taken any particular notice of him. He was just a name on the record books—Gino Luisetti, son of Guiseppe Luisetti, who was a sewer walker.

His mother said worriedly, "You do not have enough fun, Gino. You do not play like you used to when you were younger."

"You want me to play football, Mom?" he asked.

"I do not know this football," she said. "If it will make you happy, you should do it."

"I don't know that it'll make me happy," he said.

"If you will be unhappy not to play," she said shrewdly, "then you had better play, *Bambino.*"

Gino watched a big gray cat slink along the base of a fence below, then climb the fence, and disappear on the other side.

He knew it was true that he'd not been very happy lately. He was keeping too much to himself. Aside from a very few friends like Benny Irvine, he saw no one. His classmates in school were just faces.

"Gino," his mother said softly, "you had better play this football."

❖   ❖   ❖   ❖   ❖

At three-thirty the next afternoon he was out on the soccer field with about thirty-five other hopefuls, boys mostly his own age, who were trying out for the junior-varsity team. They had been given cast-off varsity uniforms in the locker room where they had registered, and they felt awkward in the bulky shoulder pads, and padded football pants.

Benny Irvine looked twice as heavy as he was when he raced about, dancing, warming up. Whip was there, wearing a big No. 12 on his faded blue City High jersey. He was throwing the ball to another boy who came from their block. He threw easily, accurately, and Gino remembered that Whip had always been the best passer in those games they'd had in the street. He had long arms, and big hands for throwing a ball.

Gino wasn't sure, as yet, what position he'd try for. It didn't matter a great deal. He was out on the field, and he had given the lie to Whip, who had thought he was afraid to play.

He saw Whip looking over in his direction several times, but the red-haired boy didn't say anything.

Wayne McCarthy came out on the field, blew his whistle, and lined up the prospective jayvees. Across the field Gino saw the varsity working out with Coach Hannigan. They looked very big and very smooth as they went through their paces. The varsity had been practicing for nearly a week, and there were quite a few players from last year's team still on the squad.

Mr. McCarthy gave a brief talk, telling what was expected of them. He was again the hard taskmaster, unsmiling, speaking in a crisp voice. Once his hard blue eyes lingered on Gino, who was standing in the rear of the group, but he took no particular notice of him when they started doing setting-up exercises.

A good many of the boys had no idea what position they wanted to play, and Mr. McCarthy had to start from scratch. After the limbering-up exercises, he lined them up in a long row across the field for a dash from one goal line to the other.

21

Benny said excitedly to Gino, "He wants to find out who can run. Here's where you come in, Gino!"

Gino didn't say anything. He had always been able to run fast, very fast, and in this test he was quite sure he would come out ahead of most of the other boys. A good many of them were short and squat, like Benny, and they did not have the legs for running. Whip Grogan could run, though, and he would be up ahead with the leaders.

When Mr. McCarthy blew a sharp blast on his whistle, the line moved forward. Gino jumped up to the front in several quick strides. It was a hundred-yard dash, and they had to run at top speed all the way.

After the first fifty yards, Gino discovered that he was running alone, and then he saw Whip down along the line drawing up closer to him. Wayne McCarthy was watching them from the side lines, twirling his whistle on the thong, his cap pulled down over his eyes.

Gino had never run with cleated shoes before, and it felt good, digging into the dirt, driving forward. He strained every muscle, felt himself pulling ahead of Whip, and then he saw that Whip was coming up again, fighting doggedly for the lead.

Behind him, Gino heard Benny gasp, "Go it, Gino! Go on, *Italiano!*"

Twenty-five yards from the finish line, the two boys were neck and neck, with the nearest competitor several yards to the rear. Gino's legs were working like pistons as he fought to defeat the hated Whip. He strained, his chest hurting, his legs hurting, and again he pulled ahead of Whip, this time to stay there as he lunged across the broad white stripe of chalk which marked the goal line.

Wayne McCarthy walked down toward them leisurely as they pulled up. Gino looked over at Whip, and he saw the dislike in the other boy's eyes.

"Nice running," Mr. McCarthy said. "We can use fast men on any squad."

"He's used to runnin'," Whip said, nodding toward Gino, and Gino knew what he was talking about even if Mr. McCarthy didn't. Whip meant that he was used to running—*away*.

"If you two boys can play football as well as you run," Mr. McCarthy said, "we'll be able to use you on the squad. How about you, Grogan? What's your choice as a player?"

"Halfback," Whip said promptly. "Maybe quarterback. I like to pass."

Mr. McCarthy looked at Gino. "How about you, Luisetti?"

Gino moistened his lips. "I haven't thought about it," he said. "I'll try anything."

"With that speed," Mr. McCarthy told him, "you could make a pretty good end and pass receiver. Like to try for the end position?"

There was a very faint smile on the coach's face as he made the suggestion. Gino hesitated for the moment. If he were an end, it meant that he and Grogan would have to combine on the passing and receiving. They would form a team!

"Lots of action at the wing position," Mr. McCarthy was saying. "You have the build for it, Luisetti. We need rangy boys, who can run."

Gino nodded. "All right," he said.

"You'll have to get plenty of practice on pass-receiving," Wayne McCarthy was saying. "Suppose you two start in right away." He tossed a football to Whip, and then lined up a half dozen other boys to work with them.

For the next half hour Whip threw passes to boys running out from the end of the line. He threw sharply, accurately, for a boy of fourteen, and Gino saw that Mr. McCarthy was pleased.

He did well, himself, on the receiving end. He had always been able to catch a ball well, and Whip put the ball where he could catch it. Occasionally, however, when Wayne McCarthy wasn't looking, Whip threw the ball very hard, deliberately to make Gino miss it, and he grinned when the ball bounced off Gino's outstretched fingers.

There was no scrimmaging the first afternoon as Mr. McCarthy looked over the squad carefully, trying to assign different boys to the various positions. All of them had played a little football in the streets. They could handle the ball, but very few had ever played tackle with eleven men to a side.

When the workout was over, Gino trudged from the field with Benny at his side, and as he passed Mr. McCarthy standing by the door, the coach said, "How did it go, Luisetti?"

"All right," Gino nodded.

"Think you'll like it at end?"

"I'll try," Gino told him.

The squad went into the locker room, tired, worn out, but there was no booing. Gino noticed that right away. Wayne McCarthy had worked this squad the way he'd never worked a gym class, but there was no booing when it was over.

Gino walked home with Benny, and it was past five o'clock in the afternoon when they reached their block.

Benny said just before they parted, "You think you'll make the team, Gino?"

"Mr. McCarthy's trying me at end," Gino told him. "He seemed to think I'd fit in there." He looked down at little Benny and said, "How about you?"

"I don't know," Benny muttered. "There's an awful lot of fellows working out for the line."

"You'll make it," Gino consoled. "They always need a lot of linemen."

"Once they start tackling," Benny vowed, "I'll show them. Mr. McCarthy will have to notice me, then."

"Sure," Gino grinned. "You're all right, Benny."

He went on to his own house, and he was going up the steps when he saw his father coming down the street, walking heavily as usual, a short, squat, dark-faced man in old work clothes.

The father's eyes lighted up as he approached the tenement house. He wore a battered brown fedora hat, and when he came up, the smell of the sewer would be on him even though he had changed his clothes and washed when he had come up into the daylight.

Gino watched him, and he thought fiercely, *I'm not ashamed of him. Why should I be ashamed of him? He's the best man that ever lived!*

He hated Whip for his slurring remarks; he hated all people who looked down upon another man because of his position in life. There were many like Whip. He was sure of that.

THREE

The first week of practice with the jayvee team assured Gino of a position on the first team. He had a lot to learn about playing end, but Wayne McCarthy had started to work with him earnestly.

In the few scrimmages he had proved that he could tackle. He went in hard and low after his man, driving him back the way Mr. McCarthy wanted him to. He learned how to play out wide so that he couldn't be boxed in on end runs, and each afternoon he improved on pass receiving.

Mr. McCarthy put him out at the left end position, and when the jayvee regulars scrimmaged against the scrubs, he proved his value by snatching pass after pass from Whip, and making long gains.

To his surprise little Benny made first string, also. Benny did not look too good in practice until the scrimmaging started. Coach McCarthy had Benny playing with the scrubs, but after about ten minutes he was switched over to the regulars at the left-guard position. Benny was a great tackler. He held his ground, and when the runner came his way, Benny always had a hand ready for him.

He was quick, too, and quite often he managed to wriggle his way through the scrimmage line to stop the runner in his own territory.

Gino was overjoyed when Mr. McCarthy made the switch, and Benny came over to the regulars.

"Teammates," Benny grinned. "We'll show 'em, *Italiano.*"

They had their first game of the season scheduled for the next Saturday, following the varsity game earlier in the afternoon. The varsity played Washington High from the north side of the city, and the junior-varsity was to play the Washington jayvees.

The day before the Washington High game, Gino felt the excitement rising in him. It was his first real game of football with full uniform, on a regular football gridiron, and with referees, and rules and regulations. He hoped he wouldn't disgrace himself.

"We're going to use a lot of passes," Wayne McCarthy said to the team the afternoon before the game. "We have a very fine pass combination in Grogan and Luisetti, and I think we can score with it."

Whip sat across the room from Gino, rubbing his hands, looking at the floor. During the afternoons that they'd been working together on the gridiron, Whip had had very little to say. He treated Gino with the same cool contempt as before, but he'd never tried to bring anything to a head since Mr. McCarthy had stopped their impending fight.

Mr. McCarthy was saying, "We'll need a team captain when we take the field tomorrow afternoon. It's your privilege to elect the man you want."

The boys looked at each other uncomfortably, and then one boy said, "How about Johnny Anderson?"

Johnny Anderson was the fullback, a tall, blond boy, quiet, but very efficient. He didn't have much to say, but no one had ever attempted to push him around, and even Whip let him alone.

"Johnny for me," Benny Irvine said.

A vote was quickly taken, and the embarrassed Johnny Anderson was made team captain. Wayne McCarthy read off the names of the boys who were to start the Washington game, and then the meeting was over.

Gino walked home with Benny again, and this time Whip trailed after them.

As they walked down the street toward their block, Whip said, "You better catch those passes tomorrow, Ginzo. I want to make the varsity next year, or maybe even this year, and I won't unless you help me to look good."

"You throw them right," Gino scowled, "and I'll catch them, but not for you."

"Just catch them," Whip said tersely, "or else."

When he left them, Benny said, "Don't worry about him, Gino. He's mostly talk."

"I'm not worrying about him," Gino told him. He had to admit though that Whip had dampened his enthusiasm for the game. He wondered why there had to be people like Whip Grogan in the world.

✻   ✻   ✻   ✻   ✻

The Washington jayvees looked big when they came out on the field after a City High win over the varsity. They wore red and white uniforms, with bright white helmets and red and white candy-striped socks.

Gino said apprehensively to Benny, "You think we can beat them?"

"Why not?" Benny chirped. "Remember, it's their first game, too."

They were out on the field warming up, with the big crowd which had watched the varsity game still lingering for the jayvee game. Over on the side lines the varsity City High coach, Bob Hannigan, spoke with Wayne McCarthy, and the two men watched the jayvees thoughtfully.

30

Whip, as quarterback, worked the first team down the field, using some of the simple plays that Mr. McCarthy had taught them. There was no nervousness in Whip Grogan.

Gino watched him, taking the ball from Milton Gruber, the center, handing it off to one of the backs, Anderson, Lou Winfield, or Bruno Jablonski. Whip seemed to know what he was doing all the time.

As the team moved down the field in this warm-up session, Gino felt for the first time that he was part of it, not just Gino Luisetti, but one of eleven men getting ready to face a common enemy. There was power in the way they lunged forward with each handback. Gino dug his leather cleats into the torn turf and plowed ahead, driving with his legs. Once he glanced over at Benny, and Benny grinned at him.

The left tackle, Howie Benson, a tall, angular boy with a long jaw, said, "We'll get 'em, Gino."

Gino looked down along the line. There were Benson, Benny Irvine, and Milton Gruber, the center. Then the other side of the City High line, Joe Basilo, right guard, Wally Corwin, tackle, and Charlie Brock, the right end. These were the boys who had fought for the positions and clinched them for this opening game.

After awhile the whistle blew. Johnny Anderson went out to the toss-up with the Washington captain, and he won the toss, electing to receive. The eleven City High jayvees scattered across the field, Gino along the left side line.

For the first time the panic hit him, and he wondered what he would do if the kick was bad and wobbled over in his direction. On the kickoff he was supposed to block the Washington boys coming down at him.

The kick went high into the air, falling into the hands of Lou Winfield, the left halfback. Gino took one look at the ball, and then started forward, running directly toward a Washington boy in a red jersey and a white helmet.

The boy tried to get out of his way, but Gino lunged in hard and low, upsetting him. He heard the noise around him as the play swept by. Benny had knocked down a Washington player, also, and Lou Winfield carried the ball up to mid-field, a very fine runback.

The first huddle was different from the huddles they'd had on the practice field, working against the scrubs. This was the real thing.

Whip called the play in a crisp voice, and it was to be a straight hand-off to Johnny Anderson, and a plunge over left guard. On the play Gino was to swing in wide and try to take out the Washington right halfback.

He was too anxious to move, however, and he started running before the ball was handed back on the third number. A whistle blew as soon as the play started, and although Johnny Anderson made four yards, the referee penalized City High five yards for off side. Gino had been off side.

In the huddle Whip said grimly, "Let's get into it."

He looked straight at Gino at the far end of the huddle, and Gino reddened as he stared down at the ground.

Whip had orders from Wayne McCarthy to use mostly ground plays in the beginning and to take no chances with passes. There were good runners in the City High backfield. Bruno Jablonski, the right half, was the fastest of the four backs, a small Polish boy with black hair and dark eyes. Johnny Anderson and Lou Winfield also were fast, hard runners, and Whip, when he carried the ball, could keep up with any of them.

They made nice gains through the Washington line, moving the ball down to the Washington fifteen-yard line, and then little Bruno broke loose, skipped around Gino's end, and went over for a touchdown.

It was the first score for the City High jayvees, and they whooped it up, pounding Bruno's back after he came back, grinning, the ball under his arm.

Gino had gone through to knock down the Washington right half on the play, clearing the way for Bruno.

The little Polish boy yelled, "Nice work, Gino."

Gino grinned at him. Benny came over and said, "Some team, Gino."

Gino nodded. It was some team, he thought. Even with Whip on it, it was some team.

Those first few minutes he had done nothing but block for the runners, but now Washington would have the ball on the kickoff, and he would be on the defensive. He had to make tackles and stop the runners coming around his end.

He had come to like this part of the game, too. It was a matter of pride with the boys on the left side of the City High line that the opposing runners made no gains on their side.

After the kickoff, Washington tried its first running play, with the left halfback coming around Gino's side. Gino heard Benny yell the warning. He saw the blockers swinging out wide, and the runner coming with the ball under his arm, running hard, his face tense.

Little Benny lunged in at them, reaching for the runner, and missed. Howie Benson was in close also, but one of the blockers knocked him down.

Gino, remembering Mr. McCarthy's orders, kept

moving out farther and farther, trying to push the runner in toward the center. When he saw his chance, he leaped in low, reaching for the runner's legs. He didn't stop the boy but tripped him so that he fell forward awkwardly, and Milton Gruber, the center, coming up fast, was able to make the tackle.

Gino got up, breathing hard. The runner had made about a yard on the play, and he'd been stopped because Gino was able to get a hand on him.

On the second play a Washington runner tried to go through Benny's position, and Benny sneaked through to tackle him behind the line of scrimmage for a two-yard loss.

The City High jayvee line yelped happily after Benny made the tackle. They were holding Washington, and it felt good.

Gino had the feeling that they were going to try his end again, and he moved out a little wider, crouching, watching the Washington huddle. He saw one of the halfbacks glance surreptitiously in his direction, and he edged a little closer to the line of scrimmage.

The play was supposed to be a fake hand-off to the fullback, and then the real hand-off to the right half coming around from the rear. Something went wrong though after the fake. The quarterback jammed the ball too hard at the runner, and he fumbled it.

Darting in, Gino saw the pigskin bouncing loose on the ground, and he heard the excited yells from the boys of both teams. A red-jerseyed Washington boy was running after it, trying to pick it up, but the ball kept bounding away from him, and then Gino went forward in a long, low dive, reaching for the ball.

When it struck his chest, he got both arms around it and held tight. Two Washington players plumped down on top of him, and the whistle blew loudly.

"Gino!" Benny whooped. "Hey—Gino!"

Gino got up with the ball in his hands and gave it to the referee. The other City High boys were pounding his back, and he grinned sheepishly.

"Let's go," Whip said gruffly in the huddle.

They started to move again from the Washington thirty-yard line. Johnny Anderson made two yards over center, and Bruno Jablonski made three yards around the right end.

On the third play Whip said, "Pass—11-P." He looked at Gino significantly. It was a pass play to Gino, a short pass over the center, one they had practiced steadily since the passing combination had been established.

The team lined up, and Gino played out wide, staring straight ahead of him. When the snap number came, he darted forward, running straight for several paces and then swinging in toward center.

Whip's short pass came straight at him, plunking against his chest. He was running fast when he caught the ball, and he kept going, turning down toward the goal line and then breaking past a Washington line-backer.

Quite suddenly he found himself out in the clear, and he heard boys whooping behind him. The goal line was less than twenty yards away with no one in front of him.

"Go it, Gino!" Benny was howling. "Run!"

He really did run then, his legs moving, the ball tight under his arm. He saw a Washington boy angling across the field toward him, running hard, but he ran a little harder himself, flashing over the goal line for a touchdown.

Wayne McCarthy was grinning on the side lines, and even Whip looked quite pleased that his pass had resulted in a score for City High.

Benny came up to pound Gino's back. The other boys gathered around him, yelling. Johnny Anderson shook his hand and said it was a great run. The score was 13-0 for City High. They missed the extra point kick.

At the end of the half it was still 13-0 for City High, with Washington tightening up and beginning to make ground, themselves. They were nervous and unsettled in the early part of the game, and now they started to show their true worth.

Twice in the final minutes of the first half they pushed the ball deep into City High territory, losing a score only when they fumbled on the six-yard line, and Benny Irvine recovered.

In the dressing room between halves Mr. McCarthy said quietly, "They'll be coming strong the next half, and you'll have to be on your toes. Play it safe. We have the lead, and they have to score the points."

Gino sat on the bench in the locker room, looking at the sweaty, dirt-stained faces of the players. He felt good here this afternoon, better than he had ever felt in his life. He had made his score for City High, his school, and he had made a number of good tackles on the defense. Next half he would be even better.

They went out onto the field and kicked off to Washington. The Washington jayvees started off with a bang as soon as they had possession of the ball. The right side of the City line was not too strong, and the opponents began to pound there, making long gains.

Five minutes after the half had commenced, they went over for their first score. The extra point kick was good, and the score was 13-7 for City.

Benny looked at Gino and shook his head. The game wasn't going the way they had thought it would go in those early minutes. It was going to be a real fight from now on.

Washington kicked off, and little Bruno Jablonski dropped the ball when it came to him. He picked it up hurriedly and dropped it again, and then a Washington player hit him as he was recovering it the second time.

City put the ball in play on their own thirty-yard line, and on the first play Lou Winfield fumbled a hand-off from Whip, and an alert Washington boy fell on the ball.

Unnerved again, City went on the defense, but it was not the same City team which had overrun Washington High in the first quarter. They were worried now, and only little Benny kept up a chatter as they prepared to fight off this Washington attack.

Washington fooled them on the first play. With the City line and backfield looking for running plays, the Washington quarterback faded and threw a long pass to his left end, who had gotten beyond little Bruno playing safety.

The end caught the ball on the ten-yard line and kept running across the goal line for the score. The Washington rooters went wild as the score was tied up, and they cheered even more loudly when the extra point kick was successful and they led by a 14-13 score.

"We'll get 'em," Benny kept saying. "Don't worry. We'll get 'em."

Gino wasn't too sure now. Washington was playing heads-up football, and they would not be stopped. They'd come from behind to take the lead, and they were confident, while City had lost much of its confidence.

Wayne McCarthy sent in a few substitutions to see if he could check this Washington drive, but the new boys were very nervous, too; it was their first game, and they made mistakes.

Near the end of the third quarter, when Gino was sitting on the bench, having been taken out for a rest, Washington nearly scored again. They went over for the touchdown on a nice run by the fullback, but the play was called back on an off-sides penalty.

Back into the game in the fourth quarter, Gino prayed that he would be able to do something to put City ahead again. Washington had the ball most of the time now, and there were few opportunities.

The City High rooters were yelling for a score as the fourth quarter got under way. Mr. McCarthy had given Whip orders to start passing now as soon as they got possession of the ball.

Whip tried one pass, and a Washington boy intercepted it. The gloomy City High team went on the defensive again, and even little Benny this time was quiet.

Confident of victory now, Washington played careful football, taking no chances. In these closing minutes of the game they had but to hold on to that one point lead, and the victory would be as sweet as if they'd won by one hundred points.

With less than two minutes of the game remaining, City High had its break. It was fourth down and six to go on the Washington thirty-eight yard line, and Washington lined up in kick formation.

From the City bench came cries of, "Block the kick—block the kick!"

Gino tried mightily to get past the blockers and at the kicker, but two men held him off. A City High boy was going through, a small boy in faded blue City jersey.

Gino caught a glimpse of him fighting his way around the Washington fullback, and when the ball was kicked, the small boy took it against his chest. There was a big yell from the City rooters, and the small boy tore after the bounding ball which had bounced back in the direction of the Washington goal line. The small boy was Benny Irvine.

Gino found himself yelling like mad with the others as Benny fell on the ball on the Washington twenty-one yard line. It was first and ten for City, with the goal line twenty-one scant yards away.

It was the big chance they had been waiting for, and there was time for only a few plays at most.

In the huddle Whip said, "We'll pass. 14-P."

Gino gulped. 14-P was his play, a long pass down the left side line.

"Hold it," Whip said gruffly.

Then they moved to their positions, Gino crouched out wide, his heart pounding, feeling suddenly weak. In the early minutes of the game it had not mattered so much. You could make a mistake, or do something wrong, and the game did not depend upon it. Now they had time for another play or two, and if it failed they lost.

He felt the sweat break out on his face, and his hands were clammy. He heard Whip calling the numbers, and on the third number he started to run automatically. He went straight forward, running fast, and then he turned and cut for the side lines, striving to get behind the Washington safety man who was crossing over to cover him.

When he was past the ten-yard line, he turned his head to look back, and he saw Whip with his arm drawn back, ready to throw. Two red-jerseyed boys were closing in on him fast, but Whip got the ball away—a long, spiraling pass down the field.

Gino kept running, getting past the safety man, into the end zone, and the ball was dropping toward him. He turned, holding up his hands, scarcely breathing now. He was in the clear, and in the end zone, and over the goal line. All he had to do now was to catch the ball, and City High had won its first game.

The ball kept getting bigger and bigger. He heard the noise, the suddenly triumphant shouts from the City High side of the field, and then the ball struck his chest. He drew his arms and hands together to hold it, but something happened. The ball wasn't there any more. Somehow, some way, it had gotten away from him. It was bouncing on the grass, bouncing away from him, and the quick cheers of triumph were cut off suddenly.

The gun had banged from the side lines, ending the game, as the ball struck his chest. City High had lost.

For one long moment Gino stood there, staring after the bounding ball, and he died inwardly. The City players were looking at him, still petrified, unable to believe that they had come so close to victory only to have it elude them.

Gino started to walk woodenly toward the bench. He wanted to get away now, to hide, to lose himself. He wanted to cry, but he couldn't. He could do nothing but walk, and walk, and wish he were dead.

FOUR

The first boy that Gino saw on Monday morning after the Washington game was Johnny Anderson, captain of the jayvees. Gino had left the locker room early right after the game, going home alone, heedless of Benny Irvine's call to wait for him.

It was a glum, silent locker room with only Mr. McCarthy talking, trying to cheer them up. They had lost, but they were not disgraced; they had played good football, and they had been up against a good team.

Gino thought at first that he would avoid Johnny, but the jayvee captain walked straight toward him, lifting a hand as he came up. He said quite cheerfully, "How's it, Gino?"

Gino glanced at him as he fell in step, and they walked down along the school building together. He knew what Johnny thought of him, and he knew what the others thought of him. He had lost a game they should have won, and they had their opinion of him.

"Next Saturday, Metropolitan High," Johnny was saying. "That one we're going to win."

"Maybe, if I sit on the bench," Gino said, experimentally.

"You're crazy," Johnny laughed. "I heard Mr. McCarthy say that you played a whale of a game."

"And I lost it, too," Gino pointed out.

"Just because you dropped that pass?" Johnny asked, slowing down. "Don't be silly. Anybody can drop a pass. Why even the big pro players drop passes."

Gino moistened his lips and said nothing as they entered one of the school doors and moved down the corridor toward English 2, which was their first class of the day.

There were several other boys from the jayvee squad in English 2, and when they saw Gino they waved and grinned. Gino sat down on his seat, dazedly. He expected the cold shoulder today; he expected even curses, and they were treating him as if nothing had happened!

There was a nice feeling among the members of the football squad. They'd been through something together, and it did make a difference. They were no longer just boys attending City High, only faintly

45

aware of each other. They were the *team*. When you belong to the team, you no longer walk alone.

Benny Irvine came in and sat down across from Gino, plunking his books down on his desk in disgust. The English teacher wasn't in the room as yet, and they could speak freely.

"Where were you over the weekend, Gino?" Benny wanted to know. "Were you hiding under a rock or something?"

"I—I was busy," Gino said.

"Well, don't do it again," Benny scowled.

It was different, going from one class to the other now. Every change period, Gino would see some of the boys from the squad in the corridor, and they would wave and grin, and pass each other, or fall in step and discuss the game of the previous Saturday—all except Whip Grogan.

Twice during the morning session Gino passed Whip in the hall, and Whip just stared at him contemptuously. Whip had thrown that pass which Gino had dropped, and if Gino had caught it, much of the glory would have fallen upon Whip Grogan for his successful throw.

"Don't worry about him," Benny said. "Whip's just sore at everybody. I don't think he even likes himself."

When they reached the gym class in the afternoon, however, the change was really noticeable.

None of the jayvee boys booed Wayne McCarthy from the locker room, and they even tried to get some of the other boys to stop it.

Gino noticed that Whip wasn't booing either, the way he had those first few weeks of school. Whip sat down at the other end of the bench, and once or twice he started to sniff and look around.

Benny said softly, "Don't say anything, Gino. Just forget about it."

They went out on the gym floor, and Mr. Mc-Carthy put them through their calisthenics. All the while Gino was wondering how the jayvee coach felt about his fumble of that pass on Saturday. He had not seen Mr. McCarthy since the game. There had been a lot of confusion in the dressing room, and the coach had been outside talking with the varsity coach.

Gino stared straight ahead of him as he went through the exercises, but as they were leaving the floor after dismissal, Mr. McCarthy was waiting for him near the door. He said as Gino was about to pass him, "How'd it go Saturday, Gino?"

Gino stopped. "I lost the game," he said. "You saw it."

Wayne McCarthy shook his head. "No one man loses a football game, and no one man wins it, Gino. Always remember that. There were a half dozen instances during that game on Saturday when I

47

could have said it was lost, and a particular player lost it, but we never figure that way. Eleven men on the field lost it; you were one of the eleven men, and you played good football, Gino. Keep it up."

He put a hand on Gino's shoulder and walked off, and Gino went into the locker room, trembling with happiness. No one had ever talked to him like that before.

All day he had been considering dropping from the squad, but now he was going to stay. He was going to play some real football for Mr. McCarthy.

In the locker room though it was different. Whip had seen him pause to speak with Mr. McCarthy, and Whip wasn't going to let this go by.

"Pretty chummy with the coach, aren't you, Ginzo?" he asked.

"Never mind," Gino growled.

"You lost the game last week," Whip said, "and you have to be pals now so he won't throw you from the squad. That the way it works?"

"He never said anything about throwing me from the squad," Gino snapped.

Little Benny took Gino by the arm. "Come on," he said. "We have to go."

They went on to the next class, and at three-thirty they were out on the field for practice. Saturday's defeat was forgotten as they prepared for the next game the following Saturday.

48

Mr. McCarthy worked them hard, drilling them in football fundamentals. The tackling and the blocking had been very sloppy in that first game, and he lined up two squads of boys in front of the tackling dummy.

For almost an hour they hit the dummy with tackles and with blocks, with Mr. McCarthy showing them how to get their weight behind the tackles and to dig when they made contact.

"When you've committed yourself to a tackle or a block," Mr. McCarthy said, "don't hesitate, and give it all you've got. More boys are hurt because they change their minds after they've started to make a tackle. When you're going in, keep going, and go hard."

The afternoon was hot, and they perspired freely before it was over, but there was no grumbling.

"A good team must know how to tackle and block," Wayne McCarthy told them. "If you can't do that, you don't have it."

Near the end of the session the regulars went through some of the plays they had used against Washington on Saturday, and again Mr. McCarthy pointed out their mistakes.

"It's all in the timing," he explained. "Your play has to go 1-2-3. A blocker hits his man, and there's a hole for a split second. The ball is handed to the back, and he's through. You delay a fraction of a second on the hand-off, and the hole might not be there any more."

Whip Grogan was in for some high praise for his handling of the squad. Whip was a natural quarterback, making very few mistakes. He was smart and confident, two assets every quarterback must have. He never got rattled in the game, and he was a fine schoolboy passer.

"We'll use more passes against Metropolitan on Saturday," Mr. McCarthy said. "I wasn't too sure about them last week. It's a quick way to make ground, but you can lose the ball very quickly, too."

When Wayne McCarthy was out of hearing, Whip said, "We'll make the ground if the receivers hold on to the passes. You have one of those Ginzos at the other end who clams up when the ball's coming at him, and you'll never make any ground."

Johnny Anderson, who was close by, looked at Whip steadily, and then he said, "We don't want that sort of stuff on this squad, Whip. Why don't you cut it out?"

"Who lost the game last week?" Whip demanded. "I put the ball right in his hands over the goal line. He got scared because they were coming at him."

"Anybody can drop a pass," Johnny said quietly. "You'll make fumbles, yourself, before the season is over."

"When I make a fumble like that," Grogan grinned, "I'll drop dead."

He walked away, and Johnny said to Gino, "Don't let him get you worried, Gino. You played a great game, Saturday."

"Thanks," Gino murmured.

He looked around at the rest of the boys who'd heard the altercation, and it was apparent that all of them were on his side. Whip had always been too high-handed, and too quick with his tongue and with his fists. He wasn't popular on this team, even though everyone knew he was a fine player, probably the best on the squad.

They had no more trouble the remainder of the afternoon, Mr. McCarthy keeping them at it till five o'clock. When they went home after taking their showers, they were tired boys.

Whip had left a short while before Benny and Gino, and they saw him as they reached their block. He was standing out in front of Sam's Candy Store with a group of older boys, sixteen- and seventeen-year-olds.

"You know who they are?" Benny said as they went past on the other side of the street.

"Who?" Gino asked.

"Some of the Barons," Benny told him. "That's a new street gang just started up. Rocky Morano runs it, and you know how tough he is."

Everybody on the block knew about Rocky Morano. Rocky had been in reform school for several years, and he was out again. He hadn't gone back to high school, and as far as anyone knew he didn't have a job, but he was always around, a heavy-set, dark-haired, blunt-nosed boy with small black eyes. Rocky was seventeen, three years older than Whip Grogan.

"If Whip hangs around with a crowd like that," Benny said, "he'll be getting into plenty of trouble. My father says the police are watching them now. There have been a few robberies in the neighborhood, and he thinks the Barons are behind them."

"You don't think Whip's in the gang?" Gino said incredulously. "He's too young."

"I don't think he's in now," Benny told him, "but he's been hanging around Rocky."

"If he joins a gang like that," Gino said, "he's crazy. My father always told me to stay away from that bunch."

"Mine, too," Benny nodded. He added thoughtfully, "It won't do the team much good if Whip gets in trouble and can't play any more. We need Whip."

"Do we?" Gino asked grimly.

Benny looked at him. "Sure," he said. "You know that. Whip's a good quarterback."

Gino was thinking how nice things would be if Whip Grogan were not around to make remarks and to goad him. He could almost like it at City High.

"Whip's on the team," Benny was saying. "You know what I mean, Gino? We're all together now."

"We weren't together back in the locker room this afternoon, and on the field," Gino observed.

"That's different," Benny said. "Maybe we can fight each other a little, but when we get against somebody else, we're all for City High."

Gino just shrugged as they walked along. This was a new concept to him. It seemed kind of silly putting the school ahead of himself. City High had done nothing for him; as a matter of fact until he went out for jayvee football, he almost hated the place.

With Benny it may have been different. Benny was an eager-beaver; nothing seemed to bother him. It was conceivable that he could even like Whip Grogan if he had to. Gino knew *he* could never be like that.

*   *   *   *   *

During the remainder of the week they worked hard for the Metropolitan game, and on Saturday they were in good shape, and tremendously improved over the team which had faced Washington's jayvees.

Day by day Gino had noticed the difference. The linemen and the backs became more confident as they learned their various assignments. Wayne McCarthy worked with individual players—with the tackles, with the guards, with the two ends, teaching them little things which would help them against an opponent.

Gino learned how to throw his body across the path of an oncoming tackler who was running at top speed. Mr. McCarthy taught him how to feint when he ran out for a pass so that the secondaries could not follow him.

"Whip is a fine passer," McCarthy said. "If you can get into the clear, he'll give you the ball. We're going to depend a lot upon these passes during the remaining games on our schedule."

"Yes, sir," Gino said, but there was little enthusiasm in his voice.

If he had been teaming up with Johnny Anderson or Bruno Jablonski, it would have been different. He would have liked that, and worked hard at it, but working with Whip was not pleasant and never would be.

Against Metropolitan High the following Saturday, the passing team of Grogan and Luisetti went into action in the first five minutes of the game.

Metropolitan was not so strong, and not so alert as Washington had been. With the ball on the City

High forty-five-yard line, Whip called for a pass in the huddle.

Gino sprinted down the field, feinted to the right, and then cut sharply toward the side lines the way Mr. McCarthy had taught him. Whip's pass came at him, a long, smooth spiral, and he took it over his shoulder on the dead run, having gotten past the Metropolitan safety man.

After that it was only a matter of running fast, and he could do that. It was the second touchdown he had scored for City High, and this time on a long forty-yard run down the field.

The crowd cheered wildly as he went over the line for the first score of the game, and the City High jayvees rushed down the field to pound his back.

"Gino!" Benny whooped. *"Italiano!"*

"He can run," Johnny Anderson grinned. "They never catch him when he gets moving."

Gino saw Whip strutting around, flexing his arm, smiling in a satisfied manner. Whip's pass had been perfect on that play, just enough arch to it, and not too hard so that it would be difficult to handle.

Johnny Anderson kicked the extra point, and it was 7-0 for City High.

It didn't stay that way for long, however. As soon as City got possession of the ball again, Bruno Jablonski broke off right tackle, and ran like a scared deer sixty yards to the goal line for the second score, making it 13-0.

Confidence grew in them, then. They were winning, and they had power, and they knew it.

Whip became a little too cocky after that, and his first pass intended for Gino sailed into the hands of a Metropolitan secondary, stopping what would have been another drive for the Metropolitan goal line.

However, Benny Irvine recovered a Metropolitan fumble a few minutes later, and they were off again. Wayne McCarthy sent in orders that they should concentrate for a while on the ground attack because they needed the practice, and the backs started to reel off yardage.

Johnny Anderson, a really strong runner, plowed down the middle; Lou Winfield and Bruno Jablonski hit the ends and the tackles, and they rolled down the field with scarcely any effort.

Gino had all blocking assignments for a while, and he liked this part of the game, too. It was a pleasure swirling in behind the Metropolitan line to dump a line-backer so that Johnny or Bruno could make longer gains. He liked working for them.

They scored a third time, Johnny going over from the five-yard line on a straight plunge, and when they left the field at half time the score was 20-0 for City.

Varsity coach Bob Hannigan was in the locker room when the jayvees trooped in, flushed and happy, and Gino heard the head coach say to Wayne McCarthy, "Looks like you have a real juggernaut here, Wayne. Congratulations."

"They're playing good football," McCarthy smiled.

They played even better football in the second half. Whip started to throw passes again, on McCarthy's orders, alternating with Gino and Lou Winfield on the receiving ends, and they chewed off the yardage in big chunks.

Gino caught two in a row, good for about fifteen yards apiece, and the Metropolitan team, harried and flustered, called time out to think it over.

The grinning City team gathered in a group on the Metropolitan thirty-yard line, and the orders were to keep on passing.

"We'll drive them crazy," little Benny chuckled. "They don't know which way the ball is coming."

On the first play after the time out, Whip faked a pass to Gino, and threw it to Lou Winfield, and the ball was down on the ten-yard line.

In the huddle Gino confidently expected that Whip would call his number to receive the next pass, a touchdown pass, and he was a little stunned when Whip repeated the same play—the fake, and the pass to Lou Winfield.

He wasn't too sure either that he was pleased when the play succeeded, and Lou caught the ball in the end zone for another City score. Everyone else seemed to be happy, however. They yelled and they pounded Lou's back, but Gino had the feeling that it should have been his back they were pounding.

He glanced over at Whip, but Whip was grinning as usual, pleased with himself that he had thrown another touchdown pass.

"26-0!" Benny yelled. "What do you think of that, Gino?"

Gino nodded, and managed to smile as they lined up for the extra point kick, but he wasn't happy. He knew that Whip had deliberately given that score to Lou because he hated Gino Luisetti, and Whip, as quarterback, made all the decisions on the field. If Whip didn't want Gino to score, he just didn't call Gino's play when they were· in scoring territory. It was as simple as that, but it was not going to be so very nice. Already, Gino had been fancying himself as the leading scorer. He led with Bruno, with two touchdowns apiece, and he should have had three if Whip had played it fair.

The old feeling came back again. He wasn't playing with a team; he had to do it, himself, and they were all against him. It was like it had been before.

He didn't score any more that afternoon as Metropolitan tightened up, but City High won by a score of 26-0, their first win, and the team was jubilant as they trotted into the locker room to change.

"A great game," Benny kept saying. "A really great game. We had it this afternoon."

"We won," Gino said, and he was still thinking about that play Whip had called which gave the touchdown to Lou Winfield. It wasn't fair that one player should have the right to decide who makes the touchdowns; it especially wasn't fair when the man who had the right didn't like one of the boys on the squad.

Gino said quietly as he sat down on the bench in front of his locker and started to take off his cleats, "You notice anything funny about that pass Whip threw to Lou, the last score we made?"

"Funny?" Benny repeated. "What do you mean? It was a good pass. Lou was out in the clear."

Gino frowned. "I don't mean it that way," he said.

"How did you mean it?" Benny asked, mystified.

"Oh, just forget it," Gino scowled. "I just thought it was funny. That's all."

"I don't care whether it's funny or otherwise," Benny grinned, "as long as it's our score."

Gino thought about that for a moment. Benny as a guard probably never would make a score for

City High as long as he played for the team, jayvee or varsity. The only way a guard could score was to recover a fumble over the goal line.

This didn't seem to make much difference to Benny, however. He was in under every pile-up, and very few people noticed him. He would make a tackle on a line play, or he would open a hole for a runner; he would get a hand on a runner going through and trip him up or slow him down so that another player could make the tackle, and few people ever knew about it. Maybe Wayne McCarthy saw it, or his fellow players saw it, but that was all. There was no glory in playing guard, very little back-pounding, but Benny Irvine didn't seem to mind. He still liked to play.

Gino was sure he wouldn't have minded too much either if Whip hadn't been the one who was trying to put him down and stamp on him all the time.

He did feel bad about it, though. He should have had three touchdowns now instead of being tied with Bruno with two each.

FIVE

That Saturday night, after the Metropolitan win, Saul Irvine's tailor shop was broken into and the cash register robbed of over fifty dollars.

Benny told Gino about it on Sunday afternoon. His father had, of course, reported the robbery to the police, and detectives had come around to investigate.

"They can't prove it," Benny said grimly, "but I'll bet it was the Barons. They broke in through the rear door of the store."

Gino said slowly, "You don't think Whip was with them?"

"No," Benny shook his head. "He still doesn't belong to the gang. I know Joey Brubaker, and his brother is a Baron. He says Whip isn't in the gang."

Gino didn't say anything to that, but the thought

occurred to him that if Whip did join the Barons and got into trouble, he, Gino Luisetti, would have nothing to worry about any more.

"He's crazy even hanging around with that crowd," Benny said. "Whip can be a great football player someday if he watches himself."

Gino kept his thoughts to himself, but he was a little puzzled as to why Benny was so concerned about a boy who had always treated him roughly, and who insulted him on every occasion. Of course that was Benny's concern, but Benny seemed to think it was the concern of all of them, of the City High jayvee team. Gino didn't see it that way at all.

* * * * *

On Monday afternoon, practice started again, and with two games under their belts the City High jayvees presented an entirely different squad from the group of boys who had come out for opening practice. They carried themselves like football players now. They went through their warm-up exercises without Coach McCarthy having to tell them. The A squad and the B squad worked separately until Wayne McCarthy called them together for scrimmage, and all of the B boys looked enviously across the field at the regulars on A squad.

The following Saturday they were to play a strong Houston High jayvee squad which had already

played and won three straight games. Coach Mc-
Carthy worked hard, preparing his team for this
game.

There were new plays to be learned this week,
more complicated plays than they had used in the
first two games, and again the blocking and the
tackling had to be sharpened.

"A play is only as good as its blocking," Mr.
McCarthy told them. "No matter how clever it is,
and no matter how smooth your ball handling and
running, it's the blocking which will give you the
gains. We want good, hard blockers on this squad."

A squad was down at the far end of the field,
hitting the dummy with blocks and then practicing
blocking against each other, when the trouble broke
out between Gino and Whip.

Wayne McCarthy was with the B's, trying to
help a few misfits. The A squad was lined up in
front of the tackling dummy, charging it one at a
time, the players throwing their bodies across the
dummy in mock block.

Gino hit the dummy with a rather clumsy block
on one occasion, and when he came back down the
line, Whip said to him, "That's not as much fun as
scoring touchdowns, is it?"

Gino stopped and looked at him, his face redden-
ing.

"What does that mean?" he asked thickly.

"You know what I mean," Whip told him. "You like to be the hero on Saturdays. You like to score those touchdowns."

"You're a rotten liar," Gino said slowly.

It was then that Whip leaped forward, slashing at him with both hands. Gino held his ground, swinging back at Whip. He felt one of his fists land solidly. Then something hit him in the mouth, and he staggered backward, the taste of blood in his mouth.

He didn't fall down, but as he started to charge in again at the cool, contemptuous Whip Grogan, Johnny Anderson, Lou Winfield, and several other boys moved in between them, stopping the fight.

"We can't have this on the team," Johnny said quietly. "You both should know better than that."

"Here comes Mr. McCarthy," Benny said quickly. "Break it up."

The jayvee coach had already seen the exchange of blows, however, and he was coming on steadily, his cap pulled down low over his eyes.

When he came up, he said without any emotion, "Grogan and Luisetti, go to the locker room and take off your uniforms. Wait for me in the office, and no more fighting or you're both dropped from the squad."

The squad watched silently as the two boys turned and walked toward the school building, keeping about a dozen feet apart. They said nothing to each other as they entered the locker room, walking to their individual lockers which were on opposite sides of the room.

Gino waited until Whip had taken his shower, and then he had his shower and dressed slowly, not wanting to sit in the office with Whip across from him.

When he heard the team trooping in fifteen minutes later, he went into the office. Whip was there, completely at ease. He said, "Didn't think you had it in you to swing back, Ginzo."

Gino said nothing. His mouth was puffed, and Whip had a small cut on his right cheek as a memento of the occasion.

They were sitting on opposite sides of the room when Wayne McCarthy came in, took off his cap, and hung it on a peg on the wall. He stared at both of them for a few moments in silence, and then he said, "This has been coming a long time, hasn't it, boys?"

Whip shrugged. "You don't like a guy, you don't like a guy," he said. "That's all there is to it."

"There's more to it than that," Mr. McCarthy said tersely, "and the conditions are considerably changed now. You're both playing on the same football squad; you're both valuable players. You owe it to the others, as much as to yourselves, to put down personal differences. We can't have a team with two of the boys fighting each other."

"Won't be much of a fight," Whip grinned.

Mr. McCarthy looked at him. He said slowly, "I suppose you think that if I let you fight, that will settle everything. You'll have it out, and then you'll shake hands, and you'll be friends forever. Let me tell you that it doesn't work out that way."

Whip looked bored, but Gino was listening closely. He had been wondering, himself, if that wasn't the best way out of it. Whip obviously had it in for him. If he fought Whip, then Whip might change and be decent. Now he wasn't too sure.

"You'll have to settle your differences before you fight," Mr. McCarthy was saying, "and always remember this: that while you bear a grudge against each other, you are hurting every member of the jayvee squad. These boys are trying hard; they want to win and end up with a good record for the season. You two are working against them."

Whip still looked bored, and Mr. McCarthy said too quietly, "You had better leave now, Grogan. I'll talk to you again, later."

"Thanks," Whip grinned, and he went out.

Gino sat there, thinking that Mr. McCarthy would start to censure Whip, but instead the jayvee coach said tersely, "You should know better, Gino. I blame you more than I blame Whip."

Gino stared at him incredulously. "I—I didn't do anything," he blurted out. "Whip's always been after me."

"I know about that part of it," McCarthy nodded, "but I'm talking about the football squad now. You were a little disappointed last Saturday when Whip called for Lou Winfield to take that touchdown pass instead of yourself. You felt that it was your turn to score again. Isn't that right?"

Gino looked down at the floor. "He'd just passed to Lou," he said, "and I thought the next pass would be to me."

"You didn't know," Wayne McCarthy told him, "that I'd given Whip orders to use you as a decoy a great deal in the second half, and to throw his passes elsewhere."

"What?" Gino mumbled.

"That's the truth," Mr. McCarthy told him. "I have a conference with Whip before every game, and between halves. You know about that. I try to help him select his plays, and I told him to use you as a decoy because I knew the Metropolitan jayvee coach had given his squad orders to watch you closely as a pass receiver."

Gino didn't say anything, but he realized now how wrong he'd been in judging Whip Grogan. Whip had been following orders, playing wisely, and fooling the opposition. On that touchdown play when Lou had received the pass in the end zone, there had been two boys very close to Gino, ready to bat down a pass if it had come his way.

Wayne McCarthy said slowly, "You get along with your mother and father, Gino?"

Gino stared at him. "Of course," he said.

"And they love you?"

Gino knew how much his mother and father loved him, an only son. Everything was for their *bambino.*

"Yes," he said. "They love me."

"Did you know that Whip Grogan's parents are dead, and that he lives with an uncle who is a drunkard?"

"I—I knew his parents were dead."

"It's not much fun when your parents are dead, and you're living with somebody who doesn't care for you. Isn't that right, Gino?"

"I guess so," Gino mumbled.

"Whip has had a hard time of it since he was a little shaver," Wayne McCarthy was saying. "He's had to fight everything and everybody. That's why he's so tough. Now that he's growing up he still thinks he has to fight everybody. He can't help himself. He has to be tough because—because he's afraid."

"Afraid?" Gino asked, unbelievingly.

"That's right," Mr. McCarthy smiled. "Whip is afraid. He covers it up by being tough, and some-

68

times even mean. With you it's different. You come from a good home; your parents love you. They're taking care of you. Whip doesn't have anything. Let's try to help him a little. He can't help himself."

"He won't let me," Gino said. "Whip is like that."

"Just be patient," Mr. McCarthy smiled. "Don't let him get under your skin. We'll work it out, eventually." He added thoughtfully, "And don't think too much about scoring, Gino. It's not important who makes the score in a game; it's important only that your team make it. Remember that."

"Yes, sir," Gino said in a small voice.

When he was walking home with Benny a little while later, he said slowly, "You know what makes Whip so tough, Benny?"

"What?" Benny wanted to know.

"He's afraid," Gino said, and Benny roared with laughter, but Gino knew that it was true. He wondered how it would feel this afternoon to be going home to a place where he was not wanted.

❋ ❋ ❋ ❋ ❋

He had no more real trouble with Whip after that, but their differences were not settled by any means. Whip still looked upon him with contempt, and Gino avoided the boy as much as possible. It had been a shock, however, to learn that in the Metropolitan game, Whip had been following orders, and not trying to keep Gino in his place. Gino couldn't quite get over that.

Again, they were getting ready for a tough foe on Saturday. There were only two more games on the jayvee schedule. On Saturday they played Houston High, and on the following Saturday they closed the short season against West Side High, which was always the big game of the season. Both teams were reputed to be very strong this fall.

They played Houston on the City High field following a closely-contested game between the varsities, which Houston High won. A good part of the big crowd remained for the jayvee game, hoping to retrieve something good out of this afternoon.

It was a clear, crisp fall afternoon as Houston kicked off, and immediately there was an explosion. Little Bruno Jablonski caught the kickoff, followed his blockers up the field for some distance, and then suddenly swerved and darted up along the left side line as if he were being chased by a legion of devils.

With the crowd howling, Bruno crossed line after line, the City jayvees blocking out nicely for him. Gino made a clean block of a boy coming down the field, and then remembering Wayne McCarthy's admonition, he scrambled to his feet as quickly as possible, and went after another boy.

Bruno went all the way across the goal line for

a touchdown, a thrilling eighty-yard run, and the crowd gave him a great hand as he came back, grinning.

The Houston team was big though, and aggressive, and when they got possession of the ball after the next kickoff, they started to hammer.

Gino played out wide on the left wing, crouching, dashing in as the ball was snapped, or edging his way across the field if the play came his way, waiting for his chance to dive in at the runner.

He had learned a great deal in these three weeks of training with the jayvees. He no longer committed himself by charging every time the ball was snapped, and then having the play swirl around him. He charged hard now when a pass was obvious, or when they were going around the opposite side of the line, but when they came his way, he was very wary, using his hands to ward off blockers, always trying to get the runner to go in toward center.

The Houston team made two nice gains through the line, making a first down, and on the third play they came straight at Gino, hoping to run over him for a long gain.

He bided his time, and then knifed in between two tacklers, dumping the runner before he reached the line of scrimmage. There was another boy in on the tackle with him, and when he started to get up, he noticed that the boy was Whip. Whip was backing up the line on Gino's side of the field, and he had come in very fast on that play.

For one moment both boys stared at each other as they got up, and then Whip snorted and trotted away.

They stopped the Houston drive at mid-field, and Houston kicked down to little Bruno playing at safety. Bruno carried the ball back to the City forty-yard line, and they were ready to go.

Whip handed off to Johnny Anderson, and Johnny tore through the middle for eight yards. He gave it to Bruno, and Bruno went off left tackle for six yards and a first down.

Gino saw Wayne McCarthy staring at them from the side lines. They'd never played football like this before.

The next play was a short pass to Gino, after a fake buck at the line. Gino cut over the middle, took Whip's nice pass, and kept going to the Houston twenty-yard line. He liked to run now; he liked the feel of it with the ball tight under his arm, and tacklers coming at him. He liked to drive his way through them.

Then Whip called for a quarterback sneak, and went another seven yards to the thirteen, and Houston, dazed and battered, called time out.

"We're really moving," Benny chortled. "It's the

72

blocking Mr. McCarthy taught us. It's paying off now."

Gino had noticed that, too. The boys up in the line, and the backfield men, were blocking beautifully on every play. There were holes in the line for the runners. There was downfield blocking when the runners got through the holes.

"Let's try that trick Double X," Whip grinned in the next huddle.

It was a new play Mr. McCarthy had taught them, and which they were only to use on rare occasions. Jokingly, they'd called it Double X, instead of giving it a number.

Double X started out of an ordinary run around the right end, Lou Winfield taking the hand-off from Whip, and swinging out wide. He didn't go very far, however, because he handed the ball to Charlie Brock, the right end, who was coming the other way.

Now it looked like an end-around, with Charlie swinging around the left end, but the play still wasn't completed. Charlie gave the ball back to Whip, who was crouching with his back to the line of scrimmage, and then Charlie kept going, faking his run.

Whip suddenly whirled and fired the ball down the middle of the field to Gino Luisetti, who had been going easily down the side line and then had cut for the middle.

The play worked to perfection the first time it was tried. Mr. McCarthy didn't like to use it too much because excessive ball-handling was involved, increasing the possibility of fumbles.

Gino started to run on the signal, going easily, heading for the goal line. He turned to watch as he ran, and he saw the Houston players chasing Lou, and then when Lou handed off to Charlie Brock, they turned after Charlie, who was going in the opposite direction.

Not all of them saw Charlie hand the ball to Whip as he fled by, crouching low, and they had all forgotten about Gino who was running out easily as a decoy.

When he suddenly cut toward the middle in the end zone, he was all alone. Whip whirled and fired the ball hard straight into Gino's arms. He caught it against his chest with no one near him for the second score of the game, and the City High crowd applauded lustily.

Gino had been deathly afraid that he would drop that pass after the others had executed their part of the play so perfectly, but he squeezed the ball against his chest the moment it hit, and he held on.

The extra point was kicked, and the score was 14-0 for City High.

"We're cooking with gas," Benny yelped. "Everybody keep it up."

It didn't last for too long, however. The Houston team had been well drilled, and when they were able to settle down, it became a football game.

Houston scored in the second quarter, kicking the point, and making it 14-7. They came up close to the goal line late in the first half, and then kicked a placement between the uprights from the ten-yard line, making it 14-10, and City High started to worry.

Between halves Coach McCarthy tried to quiet them down.

"They have to score the points," he explained. "Let Houston do the worrying. Just keep cool. The team that makes the mistakes will lose this game."

"Then we won't be the ones to make the mistakes," Benny smiled. "Let them do it."

Gino sat in front of his locker and listened. This was not like it had been in the previous two games. In those games he wanted to score touchdowns and have the other boys pound him on the back. That had been the best part of the game. Now he wanted City to win. That was the way Benny felt about it, and Johnny Anderson, and Coach McCarthy, and most of the others. Maybe even Whip felt that way about it!

For the first time in his life Gino felt a little ashamed of himself, and that was a good sign.

75

SIX

City High kicked off for the second half, and the Houston runner brought the ball back to the forty. Howie Benson, who played next to Gino at left tackle, went through to make the tackle.

Then Houston started up again where they had left off in the first half, pounding the line, making long gains, and the City High jayvees didn't know how to stop them.

Houston moved down to the City twenty and then the ten-yard line, where they fumbled, and Benny recovered for City, giving them a breathing spell. Early in the third quarter, however, Houston scored on a long pass down the field, making the score 16-14. They kicked the point, and it was 17-14.

"Have to get busy now," Benny yelped.

Wayne McCarthy sent word in that they should take to the air. City hadn't done too much passing the previous two quarters because they'd been largely on the defensive. Now, however, Whip started to throw, and even though Gino didn't like the boy, he had to admit that Whip Grogan was a fine passer.

Whip connected with Bruno for a ten-yard gain. He threw to Gino for a fifteen-yard gain, and then he threw another short pass to Lou Winfield for eight yards, and City High was on the way.

Whip's passes opened the line; the Houston secondaries fell back to cover for the passes, and Whip cleverly sent runners through the middle to pick up more yardage.

They went down to the Houston ten, starting from their own thirty-two, and then Johnny Anderson bulled through to the one-yard line on a drive over the middle.

Whip faked a pass, handed off to Bruno, and Bruno went through left tackle for the score. Gino found himself yelling crazily with the others as Bruno tumbled into the end zone and City High went ahead again.

They were all yelling, pounding each other on the back. This time it had been a team drive down the field with the passer, the receivers, the runners, and the line all in on the plays.

It was a unit working together, each boy knowing what he had to do, and doing it to the best of his ability, and Gino sensed that. He was no longer alone, fighting by himself, wary of everyone else; he was part of the City High jayvee squad, and there wasn't anybody could beat them.

"Pile it on," Benny screamed.

Whip threw more passes, twice hitting Gino for nice gains. He threw to Bruno and little Bruno ran to the Houston eighteen-yard line. Gino went out as a decoy with the Houston backfield watching him, expecting him to receive the passes, and Whip fooled them by throwing to Lou Winfield and to Bruno.

They went over again on a pass to Bruno, and the score was 28-17. This time when Bruno made the score, Gino was as happy as anybody else. He had passed a landmark in his life, and he knew it.

The final score was 35-17 for City High, Gino having scored the last touchdown on a twenty-yard pass from Whip. He made a really fine catch of the pass this time, running at top speed, and taking the ball over his shoulder in a highly professional manner.

Again, there was the back-pounding, and the yelling in his ear, and it felt good.

They trooped off the field with the City High crowd giving them a fine hand for their brilliant comeback in the second half. In the locker room Wayne McCarthy told them that they played a fine game, but that they shouldn't let it go to their heads.

On the way home Benny said to Gino, "Who can beat us now? Houston is one of the best jayvee teams in the city, and we licked the ears off them. We'll take West Side next Saturday without half trying."

Gino thought so, too, but he remembered Mr. McCarthy's words.

"Every Saturday is different," Wayne McCarthy told them. "Every team is a different team. You don't win a football game until you've played it."

"We'd better be careful not to get swelled heads," Gino smiled. "We were having a pretty tough time of it in the first half, weren't we?"

"That was before we got warmed up," Benny told him. "It takes a great team a little while to get started."

"Now you think we're a great team?"

"What do you think?" Benny countered.

Gino shrugged. "We've won our last two games," he said, "and we only have one more game on the schedule to play. If we win next Saturday, we might be called a pretty good team."

"*If* we win?" Benny repeated. "Why they say Houston is a better team than West Side, and look what we did with Houston."

Gino didn't say anything to that, but he had some slight misgivings. The other players had been talking like that in the dressing room, which was the reason Coach McCarthy had warned them to be careful.

Leaving Benny at his house, Gino walked down the block and found his father sitting on the stoop, smoking an old Italian clay pipe.

The father's dark eyes lighted up as Gino approached, and he said, "*Come stà,* Gino?"

"I had a good day," Gino told him as he sat down next to his father on the stoop.

"You win the football?" Mr. Luisetti asked, curiously.

"We won, Pop," Gino nodded. "A good game."

"That is good," the father told him. "I do not understand this football." He looked at his son carefully. "You are happy, Gino?"

"Yes, Pop," Gino smiled.

His father nodded and put a hand on his shoulder, and they sat there, and Gino was not ashamed of him. He wondered why he ever should have been. Boys like Whip had poked fun at him because they were envious of him. Whip had no father; Whip had very little of anything.

*   *   *   *   *

In school Gino noticed that it was very different also. There were boys in his classes who had seen him play, and who had cheered him on Saturday. He was known and respected as the end for the jayvee football team, and one of the top scorers.

It was nice, going through the corridors and having other boys wave to you. He wasn't looking for hero worship, but it was nice to be known. He was part of the school now, not just somebody walking through the halls.

In the locker room the gym class still booed Wayne McCarthy just as lustily, but none of the jayvee players took part in it. They had their respect for the hard-jawed physical training teacher.

Again, they were preparing for a big game on Saturday, and McCarthy worked them mercilessly each afternoon. Gino noticed that the boys could take much more now. They had become hardened in these weeks since they were out on the field each afternoon. The bouncing and the jouncing didn't seem to affect them any more. When the practice sessions were over, they no longer dragged themselves from the field but even lingered, throwing a few more passes, trying a few more punts.

Several times Mr. McCarthy spoke to them about being overconfident, but Gino could see that his talks had little effect. They had experienced that sense of power as they drove a strong Houston eleven down the field, and they couldn't get over it.

Benny Irvine said once, "I don't see what Mc-Carthy's worried about. He saw what we did against Houston when we got started. It'll be the same story Saturday against West Side. Next year most of us will be up with the varsity."

"You seem pretty sure of yourself," Gino observed.

"Why not?" Benny asked him. "We're not bragging about ourselves. We just know what we can do."

Gino shrugged it off. He had his own little problem with Whip. Since they had exchanged blows, and Mr. McCarthy had warned them, they avoided each other. Whip still was coldly contemptuous of him, and Gino kept his distance.

They did notice though that Whip was spending more and more time with the Barons. Several times in the evening Gino had seen him on the corner with Rocky Morano and others of the gang, but Benny still assured him that Whip had not been taken into the gang.

"You still think he'll join if they ask him?" Gino asked once.

"He'd be crazy if he did," Benny said, "but I have Joey Brubaker kind of keeping one ear open, and he's to let me know when they plan to take Whip into the gang."

"What can we do if he does become a member?" Gino asked curiously.

Benny looked at him steadily. "We just can't let it happen, that's all. You know how important Whip is to the team. Without his passing and quarter-backing, we wouldn't get anywhere. We have to stop it."

"How?" Gino asked.

"Well," Benny said, "we'll have to figure a way. We're going to need Whip not only for the jayvees, but for the varsity the next few years. If he's in a reform school, he's no good to us."

Gino considered that fact. Whip was the key man on the squad, and if they lost him they would be considerably weakened. Still, it did seem almost impossible to keep Whip out of the Barons and out of trouble if he had a mind to join them.

"We'll see what happens," Gino said, and he hoped against hope that nothing would happen.

They worked hard during the week for the West Side game. On Friday, Wayne McCarthy gave them a light workout to taper off for the game. He broke off practice at a quarter of five.

Gino ate his supper and was getting out a few of his school books to put in an hour of study when Benny called on him.

"Can I see you downstairs?" Benny said soberly.

Gino looked at him, and then got his coat and

went down to the street. They sat on the stoop in the dim light of the street lamp across the way.

Benny said quietly, "Well, it's happened."

"What?" Gino asked, even though he was quite sure he knew what Benny was talking about.

"Whip becomes a member of the Barons tonight, and that's not the worst part of it."

"What's worse than that?" Gino scowled.

"Joey Brubaker tells me he has to take part in a robbery as his initiation. They're going to do a job tonight."

Gino felt the sweat break out on his face. "He's crazy," he muttered. "Who are they going to rob?"

"I don't know about that part of it," Benny confessed, "but it's a fact that Whip is joining up tonight, and he's going along with them when they rob this place."

"You—you think we ought to tell Mr. McCarthy?" Gino asked.

Benny shook his head emphatically. "You can't get the grownups into this," he said. "We have to work it out some way."

"You know where they meet?" Gino wanted to know.

"In that empty store next to the baker shop," Benny told him. "They go in the back way."

"You think they're over there now?"

"That's what Joey Brubaker says," Benny told him.

Gino swallowed. "What about the police?" he asked. "If it's going to be a robbery, the police should be told about it."

"We can't prove there's going to be a robbery," Benny pointed out, "and if the police get into it, Whip is caught, and that's the end of it."

Gino looked at him. "That means there's only one thing to do."

"You know what it is," Benny said slowly.

"We have to go over there," Gino said.

"And there'll be trouble. You know that Rocky Morano will probably beat us both up."

Gino wasn't thinking about Rocky Morano; he was thinking about Whip Grogan, who didn't have a mother or father, and whose thinking was all mixed up. Whip thought he had to be tough and that he had to associate with a tough gang. Somehow, some way, he had to be straightened out, and tonight, before it was too late.

"What can you say to them?" Benny muttered. "You can't just walk in and tell Whip he can't do it."

"We'll have to walk in," Gino pointed out. "There's no other way that I can think of."

Benny grimaced. "I'm game," he said, "but they're pretty big fellows in that gang."

They sat on the stoop and Gino asked, "What time is it now?"

"About seven o'clock," Benny told him. "There's

85

no rush. They wouldn't try anything until after midnight."

"Is Whip at the meeting place now?" Gino asked.

"He's there," Benny nodded, "and so is Rocky Morano."

Gino rubbed his jaw thoughtfully. "Tomorrow we play West Side," he said, "and everything was so nice."

For the moment he considered forgetting about the whole business, and letting Whip get into trouble if he had a mind for it. After all it was Whip's life, and they didn't have to worry about him, but Whip was a teammate now, and Whip had had only misfortunes in his short life. He needed help, even if he didn't know it.

"What do you think Whip will say?" Benny asked, "if we walk in."

Gino just shook his head. He stood up, finally, and took a deep breath. "You coming?" he asked.

Benny smiled at him. "I wasn't sure what you'd do, Gino," he said softly. "I didn't want to go alone."

They walked down the street together, passing a policeman on the corner, and the policeman looked at them carefully as they went by.

"They're watching," Benny whispered when they were out of hearing. "They know about the Barons, and it's only a matter of time before they're all pulled in—Whip with them, unless we stop him."

They walked down one block and turned up another block, passing store fronts which were closed for the night. They passed groups of boys standing on the street corners, and others out in front of a poolroom. Looking at them, Gino vowed he would be different. He was taking a real interest in his studies of late. Maybe he would be able to go to college, to work his way through if he had to, but he wouldn't end up on these street corners with the other boys.

His father had often talked to him about that, mentioning college, maybe a small college where the tuition was not too high. Even though Guiseppe Luisetti was a sewer walker, he knew what was best for his boy.

When the two boys approached the empty store in which the Barons met, they both slowed down automatically.

Benny said, "We'll have to go around to the back. Joey says there's a door around there with a broken lock."

"Better go up the alley here," Gino told him, and they turned into a narrow, smelly alley a few houses before the store.

Gino saw a cat's green eyes as he went into the alley, walking carefully so that he wouldn't stumble over anything. There were tin cans and empty crates strewn in the alley, and even as they walked, a paper bag full of garbage sailed out of a top floor window, landing with a plunk in the alley.

"I don't know why they can't put it in the garbage pail," Benny scowled.

When they reached the rear of the house, they turned right, moving through several back yards, and climbing over one broken-down fence. Many of the back windows were lighted up, and they could see people in the houses, some of them still eating their suppers at the kitchen tables.

They kept back out of the light until they came up to the empty store. There was a window at the rear of the store, which had been boarded up, and the door was closed.

"This is it," Benny whispered. "You still game?"

Gino cleared his throat. "I'm still going in," he said.

They both moved toward the door together.

SEVEN

Gino felt around for the doorknob when they reached the door, and then he heard the voices inside. A crack of yellow light showed around the edge of the door. The electricity probably had been turned off in the building, and the Barons were using an old-fashioned kerosene lamp or candles.

"What are you gonna say?" Benny whispered.

Gino still didn't know. He would have to do the talking because he was the bigger boy, and it would have looked silly to stand aside and let little Benny do the talking.

His hand on the doorknob was trembling as he gripped it, and then he took a deep breath and pulled open the door.

There were five boys in the room, Whip Grogan being one of them, and the other four were all considerably older than Whip. Rocky Morano was one of them, with a cigarette in his mouth, sitting at a battered table upon which was the kerosene lamp.

Whip was sitting at the table with Rocky, and it was evident that they had been talking. All of them turned to stare at the door, and Rocky Morano stood up.

"Who's this?" Rocky said. He had a heavy, rasping voice.

Gino pushed into the room, followed by little Benny.

"Come to see Whip," Gino said, and the voice did not seem like his own.

The three boys with Rocky were all fifteen or sixteen and big fellows. One of them walked over and closed the door behind the two boys.

Whip was staring at them, a puzzled expression on his face. He asked, "What do you want?"

Gino managed to clear his throat. "Like to see you alone, Whip," he said.

Rocky Morano said evenly, "What you got to say, kid, *I'd* like to hear. Come out with it."

Gino looked at Whip.

"Go ahead and say it," Whip said.

"We don't want you to join the Barons," Gino blurted out. "We don't want you to get in trouble, Whip."

Whip stared at him, his mouth open.

"What do you know?" Rocky Morano grinned. "They don't want to see their pal get in trouble. They your pals, Whip?"

90

Whip cleared his throat. "No," he said.

"How'd you guys get in here?" one of Rocky's friends asked grimly, and he edged up closer.

"Let 'em alone, Sam," Rocky said. "I'll handle 'em when I'm ready." Then he asked Gino, "Why'd you come here if Whip didn't want you?"

Benny said, "He's on the team. Whip is half the jayvee team at City High. We don't want to lose him."

"What do you know?" Rocky murmured.

"You guys are crazy," Whip muttered. "Go on. Beat it."

Gino said, "You join the Barons, Whip, and you'll get in trouble for sure. You won't play any more football. You like to play, don't you?"

"Who sent you here?" Whip snarled, "Mr. McCarthy?"

"Nobody sent us," Gino told him. "We just came."

Whip licked his lips. "You—you just walked in?" he muttered. "Didn't you know these guys are liable to beat you up?"

"We came anyway," Gino said. "We want you to come back with us."

"Let me throw this kid out, Rocky," Sam said.

Rocky Morano said to Gino, "You that sewer walker's kid? You Gino Luisetti?"

"Yes," Gino said.

"Smell like it," Rocky grinned. "Always tell when your old man's goin' by."

Gino went white. "Don't say that," he said tersely.

"Why not?" Rocky smiled.

"I don't like it," Gino told him, his voice shaking. "I don't like you talking about my father."

"A greasy sewer walker," Rocky chuckled. "Don't get so excited, kid."

Gino walked closer to the table, his face still white, and his fists tense.

"I told you not to talk about my father," he said.

Rocky lashed out with his fist and knocked him down to the floor. Gino got up slowly, and he started to walk forward.

Whip said worriedly, "No, Gino! You'll get hurt."

Gino kept going, and when he was close enough to Rocky, he swung with his fist and missed. Rocky Morano knocked him down again, and Gino felt the blood trickling down from his mouth.

That was when Benny got into the fight. Benny, who was two heads shorter than Rocky, tore in, swinging his fists at Rocky's stomach, driving him back against the wall.

The boy called Sam yelled and lunged forward, chopping down at Benny with his fist, catching him on the back of the neck, but Benny still kept going, driving into Rocky and slamming him back against the wall.

Rocky let out a loud belch, cursed, and punched at Benny's head with both fists. Then the other two boys with Rocky jumped into the fight, one of them hitting Gino as he got up again and lunged toward Rocky.

Whip was yelling, "Stop it! Stop it! Why did you guys come in here anyway?"

It was too late to stop it now, however. Gino was swinging at everyone in sight, and Benny, who'd been knocked down, was up on his feet again, and fighting with Gino.

"City High!" Benny kept yelling. "City High!"

"Throw these little bums out," Rocky Morano snarled.

"City High!" Benny whooped.

He was hit on the side of the face by the big boy, Sam, and he went down to the dirty floor again, but he got up immediately and plunged into the fight.

"Let 'em alone," Whip muttered. "There's four against two. It's not fair."

Gino was bravely standing up against Rocky, hitting out as best he could in the dimly-lighted room, taking a good many blows in the face, but landing a few himself.

It was only a matter of moments before both of them would be badly beaten up. Rocky was angered because one of Gino's blows had caught him in the mouth and his mouth was bleeding. He started to force the fight, pushing Gino back across the room. One of the other boys came at Gino from the side, and Gino didn't know which way to go. He staggered and nearly fell, but regained his balance and tried to stand up against Rocky Morano.

"You have to let 'em alone," Whip yelled. "You hear me, Rocky?"

Rocky wasn't listening to him.

Benny was knocked down, but he jumped up, yelling, "City High!"

That was when Whip got into the fight. Whip had been standing near the table, protecting it so that the lamp wouldn't be knocked to the floor. He charged forward now, his lean face tense, and he slammed into Rocky, hitting him several hard blows, nearly knocking him to the floor, and then he whirled on the other boy.

Gino turned to help Benny, who was having a hard time of it. For the moment it was three against three, and the three smaller boys held their own. Then when Rocky got back into the fight, the pendulum started to swing the other way.

Whip yelled, "Get out. Run for the door!"

He gave Benny a push in that direction, and then the three of them tumbled out into the darkness of the back yard, Rocky Morano coming after them.

"Run!" Whip yelled.

They headed down toward the alley, scrambling

over the fences, stumbling over tin cans and rubbish. When they reached the street, they kept running, not stopping until they reached Benny's father's shop which was still open. They sat down outside, puffing, and Gino dabbed at his cut face with a handkerchief.

"I don't know why you walked in there," Whip scowled. "You knew that bunch would jump you."

"We had to get you out," Benny said. "Can't you see that, Whip?"

"Why?" Whip growled.

"You're a City High player," Benny explained, "and we need you. We're going to need you against West Side tomorrow. We didn't want to see you get in trouble and be expelled from the school."

Whip stared across the street. "What about you, Gino?" he asked slowly. "You got no use for me."

"We're on the same team," Gino told him. "We have to stick together now."

Whip didn't say anything to that.

"Were—were you going to take part in a robbery tonight?" Benny asked him.

Whip shrugged. "That's what it sounded like, but I suppose they'll change their plans now. They told me I'd have to go along with them if I wanted to get into the gang."

"Where was it to be?" Gino asked him.

"I don't know," Whip admitted. "We just got talking when you two came in."

"I'm sure glad you didn't go," Benny said.

Whip licked his lips. "Guess I'm glad I didn't go, too," he murmured. "Rocky said we'd get away with it, but he was caught before."

"They all get caught," Gino assured him, "sooner or later."

Whip rubbed his hands together and looked down at the ground.

"From now on," he said, "I'm sure of one thing."

"What's that?" Benny asked him.

"We're going to have to stick together. The Barons have it in for us, and if they catch one of us alone we might have a pretty tough time of it. If we stay together all the time, they won't have it so easy."

"Makes sense," Benny nodded.

Gino agreed, too, and when they broke up for the night, he walked with Whip down the block to their houses, Benny watching them from his shop front.

It seemed strange walking with Whip, and they didn't have too much to say to each other. When they neared Gino's house, however, Whip blurted out, "I'm glad you guys came in tonight. Did Rocky hit you pretty hard, Gino?"

"Not too bad," Gino smiled. "It would have been tough on us, though, if you hadn't joined in."

96

"They didn't have any right fighting four against two," Whip scowled. "I didn't think Rocky was like that."

"Now you know," Gino smiled.

"And another thing," Whip went on hesitantly. "I never meant those things about your father, Gino. I was just talking. You know?"

"Sure," Gino grinned. "It's all right, Whip."

❋ ❋ ❋ ❋ ❋

The next morning Benny brought them the news that Rocky Morano and three of the Barons had been caught by the police as they tried to break into a gas station on the other side of town.

"That's the end of Rocky," Benny said. "I guess we won't have to worry about the Barons any more."

"If I had been with them," Whip muttered, "I'd have gone to reform school."

They sat together on Gino's stoop, talking about it during the early morning hours. In the afternoon they were to face the strong West Side jayvees, and Coach McCarthy had asked the squad to take it easy during the morning, to relax, and to build up energy.

Johnny Anderson came up and joined them later on in the morning, and then after awhile Bruno passed by and stopped. They were all a little nervous, but sure of winning.

"After what we did to Houston last week," Benny said, "this West Side team won't stand a chance."

"I figure we'll beat them by two touchdowns," Bruno said. "Not any more."

"I wouldn't try to pick a score," Johnny Anderson pointed out. "We may find ourselves on the losing side."

"The losing side!" Benny yelped. "You crazy?"

"You haven't won a game," Johnny smiled, "until the final gun goes off."

"He has to say that," Bruno grinned, "because he's the captain."

Gino's father came out of the house, smiled at the boys, and walked down to the store. Whip glanced over at Gino, some small embarrassment showing on his face, and then he smiled.

"Still smells like the sewer," Gino said.

"Not too bad, though," Whip grinned. "That must be some job, underground all day."

"Pop's used to it," Gino told him, "and somebody has to do it."

"Better than stealing for a living," Whip murmured, and Johnny looked at him curiously.

"What does that mean?" he asked.

Whip shrugged. "I've met a few people who think they can live by stealing. That's all," he said.

"They'll find out," Johnny told him, and Whip nodded soberly.

EIGHT

In the early afternoon the sun went in, and heavy clouds scudded across the face of the sky. It turned suddenly colder, and there was the smell of rain and snow in the air.

Gino, getting into his jayvee uniform, had a glimpse of the sky from one of the windows.

He said to Benny, "It looks like we're going to get the worst of the weather after the varsity game."

The City High varsity was already in the second half against West Side, leading them by a 13-6 score, and the jayvees had gone to the locker room to dress for their game.

"I wonder how it feels playing in the snow," Benny said thoughtfully. "I'll bet the ball gets slippery."

"Have to hold on to it twice as hard," Bruno pointed out. "It's slippery enough as it is."

When the varsity came in, victorious by a 21-6 score, the rain had already started. It was as yet a light, drizzling rain but very cold, threatening to turn into snow.

Gino saw Wayne McCarthy glance up at the sky and frown as they left the locker room and trotted across the grass to the City High playing field.

"Let's give it to them," Benny whooped.

The warm-up session was cut down considerably because of the weather, and the game got under way almost immediately. City High won the toss and elected to receive.

The City High jayvees spread out across the field, and Gino was remembering how it had been in that first game he'd played. They were scared then, but now they were confident, possibly a little bit too confident.

The rain let up, and the crowd which had started to leave remained to watch. The ground was soggy, churned up by the first contest between the two varsity teams. Overhead, the sky was still dark and threatening.

The pigskin sailed out of that dark sky, and Johnny Anderson caught it and started to run. He went up to the thirty-five from the twenty-eight, and then the West Side players, wearing bright orange and black outfits, piled him up.

"Let's move it now," Bruno whooped.

They lined up in the huddle and Whip said, "14-B. That's for you, Lou."

Lou Winfield went off left tackle but didn't make any gain. The boys in the West Side line-up were pretty big, and this afternoon they were grim and determined.

Whip sent Bruno around the right end, and Bruno broke into the clear, running for twenty-five yards into West Side territory.

"That's it," Benny grinned. "We're off now."

It seemed that they were off. Whip fooled West Side by flipping a short pass to Gino, and Gino raced another ten yards down to the West Side eleven-yard line. Already, they were in scoring distance, and the game was not more than two minutes old.

They started to hammer at the middle, with Johnny Anderson and Lou Winfield carrying the ball, but the West Side line held doggedly. Johnny got down to the three-yard line but couldn't go any more, and West Side took possession of the ball.

"Block the kick!" Benny called sharply to Gino. "Block that kick."

Gino nodded. In a situation like this, West Side would probably kick on the first down to get the ball away from their goal line, and a blocked kick might mean a touchdown for City High.

The West Side kicker dropped back to kick, holding up his hands for the ball, the blockers around him, watching warily.

101

When the ball spun back, Gino tore in low the way Mr. McCarthy had taught him. He feinted one of the blockers to the left, used his hands, and went on the right side of the boy.

He saw the kicker receive the pass from center and start forward to kick it, and then he lunged in at the boy, reaching with his hands. The ball bounced off his right hand, deflecting back into the end zone.

Several blue-clad City High boys were after it, and it was Milton Gruber, the center, who finally fell on the ball in the corner of the end zone for a City High score.

"That's one," Bruno howled.

Johnny kicked the extra point, and it was 7-0 for City High.

"We'll run away with them," Benny grinned to Gino as they lined up again, this time with City High kicking off.

The kick was a bad one, wobbling off uncertainly to the right. A West Side boy picked it up and started to run. He was a slender boy with the No. 8 on his orange jersey.

Benny dived at him, and missed. Then Gino came up closer and lunged in, but the slim boy was not there. Now the West Side boys were blocking nicely, paving a path for the No. 8 boy, and he continued to run.

102

"Get him!" Bruno yelled from across the field.

The West Side boy was already in City territory, running very fast, the ball under his arm, and there didn't seem to be any City High boys near him.

Gino, getting up from the ground, stared incredulously as the slim boy kept running over the nearly obliterated white lines toward the City goal line.

Whip, who was very fast himself, got close enough to make a long dive at the boy but missed his ankles, and No. 8 went into the end zone for a West Side score.

"Boy," Benny growled, "was that lucky!"

West Side made the extra point. It was tied at seven all, with West Side kicking off again, and some more rain coming down.

The West Side kick slithered over the wet grass, going down to Lou Winfield, and Lou fumbled it after he picked it up. He managed to retain possession of the ball, but he was tackled in his tracks on the twenty-yard line.

"We go now," Whip said grimly. "Everybody ready?"

They didn't go, though. Whip called for Johnny Anderson to go into the line, but Johnny was hit before he reached the line of scrimmage. Orange-clad tacklers seemed to be coming in from all directions, and Johnny was smothered before he could get going.

A West Side boy had gone right over Benny, leaving him in the dirt, dazed and unsure of himself. Gino, blocking the West Side right tackle, had a hard time also even though Howie Benson worked with him to stop the man.

"What happened?" Whip muttered. "They were all over us before I could make the hand-off."

"We'll get 'em," Benny vowed. "Try it again."

Whip tried Bruno off right tackle, and Bruno, instead of going through this time for a long gain, was knocked down for a four-yard loss.

The West Side team was suddenly on fire, and they appeared irresistible. Whip called for another run by Johnny, and Johnny made less than a yard over right guard.

Then Johnny dropped back to kick on the last down, and he barely got the ball away. Three West Side boys were on top of him, and the ball cleared their raised hands by inches.

Gino went downfield fast with the kick, swerving in on the receiver, and tackling him just as he started to run. He nearly missed the runner because the rain was making the ground soggy, and he slipped a little as he lunged forward.

West Side started to hammer as soon as they had possession of the ball. Their backs were big fellows, and they seemed to like to run in the muck.

The rain was coming down steadily, and the West

104

Side backs piled into the line, making yardage every time. They moved slowly but relentlessly down the field into City territory, throwing no passes, and picking up the yards in small chunks.

On the fifteen, City held them for three downs, but then the West Side fullback bounced through a hole and went down to the two-yard line, where it was first and goal.

In two plays West Side was over for another score.

Gino looked at the stunned faces of the City players. They were scarcely able to believe that this was happening to them, the team which had ridden roughshod over a strong Houston High jayvee.

"Let's get going," Benny said worriedly.

It was 14-7 for West Side, with West Side kicking off again. The rain was coming down steadily, making the field a morass.

The ball was very slippery now, and when Bruno caught it on the kickoff, he nearly dropped it again. When he started to run, he slipped and fell down, and then two West Side boys hit him on the thirty-yard line.

They went into a huddle, and Whip said, "McCarthy wants us to use running plays when the ball is wet. We'll have to keep running."

"Hard to run on this stuff," Bruno muttered. "I'm slipping all over the place."

Whip tried Lou Winfield, and Lou skirted the left end, with Gino blocking hard for him, but the West Side boys seemed to be coming from all directions. Lou kept running until he was driven out of bounds for no gain.

In desperation Whip tried a quarterback sneak, got the jump on the West Side line, and went through for eight yards, a very nice gain. The City High crowd, huddled under umbrellas and newspapers, gave a cheer.

It didn't last long, however. Bruno tried to run and made two yards, and a bare first down, and then the City attack bogged down.

Whip tried two running plays which netted City exactly a yard.

In the huddle Benny said excitedly, "Why not try a pass, Whip, even if the ball is wet? They won't be looking for it."

Whip was dubious, but he was also at his wit's end. The running plays had gotten them nowhere, and there was the possibility that a pass might fool the West Side defense.

He called the play for Gino on the receiving end, and then they lined up. Gino stared straight down the field, vowing that if he caught the ball, they would never touch him until he was over the goal line for a score.

He started to run on the third number, and he cut toward the side lines, turning when he was about ten yards past the scrimmage line to look for Whip's pass.

Whip was being rushed back with the ball. There were three West Side boys on top of him, harrying him, and he had to throw hurriedly before they caught him.

The ball slithered off his hand, and Gino watched, horrified, as it fell into the hands of a West Side boy, who caught it on the dead run and kept going at top speed toward the City goal line.

"Stop him!" Gino yelled. He was out of the play, himself, having been moving in the opposite direction.

Benny saw the West Side boy coming down the side line, and he crossed over fast in an attempt to prevent the touchdown, but he slipped when he was still five yards away, and the West Side boy, grinning, kept going into the end zone for the third West Side score. They missed the extra point, but it was now 20-7 for West Side.

Johnny Anderson called time out, and the glum City High jayvees gathered down near their own goal line to talk it over. Gino could see Wayne McCarthy over on the side lines, wearing a raincoat and rain hat, staring at them, his shoulders drooping.

"What's happened to us?" Bruno muttered.

"We thought we were too good," Johnny told him grimly. "We thought nobody could lick us, and we're getting it this afternoon."

"We'll get started," Benny scowled. "It's only a matter of getting started."

"We're being outplayed," Johnny informed him. "They've got the jump on us."

"Then we'll have to get the jump on them," Gino said tersely. "We have to win this game."

He wanted to win very much for Mr. McCarthy, who was unpopular at the school, but who was fair and just, and a fine football coach. He wanted to win for City High, too, because City was his school, and this was his team.

"They're only two touchdowns ahead," Whip said. "That's not too much, and I think the rain's letting up a little."

It was true that the rain was beginning to stop, but the field was still wet, and very difficult running for fast boys like Bruno and Lou. With a wet ball, the passing also would be considerably hampered.

Time was in again, and West Side kicked off. It was a confident, aggressive West Side team which swept down the field after their kick. They had the taste of victory in their mouths, and it tasted good.

The ball went down to Lou Winfield, and Lou

managed to run ten yards before he was smothered by the orange jerseys.

Again, City tried to run with the ball, but there seemed to be no running against this big team from West Side. They tore through the line to make tackles; they piled on top of the runners before they could get started on the slippery turf, and now Whip was afraid to throw passes, having thrown one away.

The West Side defense came up close, knowing they didn't have to worry too much about Whip throwing the ball over their heads, and this made it worse for the City runners.

Johnny had to kick, and the kick was nearly blocked again. West Side put the ball in play on their own forty-five, and immediately started to hammer.

Gino fought desperately to get in at the runners. He made occasional tackles, and he was covered with mud so that he was unrecognizable, but West Side continued to advance.

Their heavier running backs plowed through the mud, and they were hard to stop. They used simple running plays with very little ball handling behind the line so that there would be less fumbling of the wet ball.

From the fifteen-yard line they went over for another score, but the play was called back for off

109

sides against West Side, and City High had a breathing spell.

Benny caught the next runner as he was coming through the line, and held on to him like grim death, preventing a first down, and City High took possession of the ball.

It was no longer the confident, unbeatable City High jayvees who started a feeble drive up the field. They were being soundly trounced, and they knew it, and there was nothing they could do about it.

Before they were up to mid-field they had to kick, and West Side took over again. It was a repetition of the first quarter with West Side riding roughshod over them, and City High digging in desperately to prevent another score.

West Side moved the ball down to the ten-yard line but ran out of time. The gun banged, ending the half just as they were getting ready to put over another score.

The teams left the field with the score still 20-7 for West Side, but everyone who had been watching knew that it could have been considerably higher.

The rain had stopped for good now, and a feeble sun was trying to break through the banks of thick clouds. A muddied, downcast squad of City High boys trooped from the field with Bruno crying openly.

Gino walked off with Whip, and he said quietly, "You think we'll be able to pass the next half?"

Whip shook his head. "We'll see what Mr. Mc-Carthy says. I think it's our only chance, but that ball is so hard to throw. I don't know how you can hold onto it either."

"I'll hold it," Gino told him, "if you get it anywhere near me."

Whip looked at him. "Okay," he said softly. "Okay—Ginzo."

"Sure," Gino grinned.

NINE

The City High dressing room was a gloomy place. Boys sat around in their muddied uniforms, heads down, knowing only one thing, that they wanted to be a thousand miles from where they were at the present time.

Wayne McCarthy came in and looked at them. Then he took off his hat and his raincoat.

He said quietly, "I've sent for clean jerseys. Everybody strip off his jersey and start to wash up—face and hands. We want a clean team to take the field the next half."

Gino heard one of the boys whisper, "A lot of good that will do. We need a new team."

"You'll feel better," Mr. McCarthy was saying, "and you'll be better. Start stripping now, and wash up. Get all that mud off your faces and hands."

Gino went over to a basin and washed his face and hands with hot water and soap. When he had finished he did feel a lot better, and when he put on one of the clean blue jerseys Mr. McCarthy had gotten for the squad, his spirits began to rise a little.

Wayne McCarthy said nothing to them until they were all washed and in the clean jerseys. He had been talking privately to Whip, however, giving him instructions as to the type of plays he had been using, and Gino saw Whip nodding his head several times.

Benny sat on his bench, the picture of despair. Benny had been the one who had been so sure of winning this afternoon, and this rout by West Side had completely bewildered him.

Gino went over and said, "We have a whole half to get back at them."

"I don't know what happened," Benny confessed. "I never thought they could do it."

Mr. McCarthy signaled for silence when word came in that they had five minutes remaining, and he began to talk then.

In a matter-of-fact voice, he said, "What has happened to this squad is not unusual. You thought you were a lot better than you are, and you ran up against a pretty tough opponent. Then the weather has been on their side, too. That makes a hard combination to beat, but it can be beaten."

"We've already beaten the first one," Benny murmured. "We know we're not as good as we thought we were."

"So now it's a new game," McCarthy went on, "only they have a thirteen-point lead. What are we going to do, lie down and die?"

No one said anything.

"The rain has stopped," McCarthy went on, "so the playing conditions won't get any worse. We may even be able to use a few passes in this half. We may win, but it won't be easy. You'll know you've been in a football game before it's over. We're starting the same team which took the field in the first half. Now go out and play football."

They went out onto the field, and the sun was shining, and they felt considerably better. The City High crowd gave them a hand, but very few people gave them a chance in this game. Gino sensed that as he took his position for the kickoff, with City High kicking off this second half.

There were relatives and friends of the players, and some of the student body which had remained behind to see the end of this game. They sat in the wet bleacher seats along the side of the field, the umbrellas folded now, grateful for the little sunshine, but without hope.

Johnny Anderson kicked off, and the West Side boy brought the ball back to the forty-two yard line. West Side picked up where they had left off in the first half.

Their heavier runners started to slam into the line.

The small boys like Benny Irvine, Joe Basilo, the guard, and Howie Benson were pushed back. They fought hard to stop the tide, and they held the orange-clad runners to small gains, but it seemed that they were always making gains.

The ball wasn't as wet as it had been the first half. The referee kept drying it with a towel after each play, and Gino considered this fact speculatively. If Whip could start to pass the way they knew he could pass—

The West Side attack stalled on the City thirty-one. They tried a long pass down the field, one of the few they'd thrown this game, and it went out of bounds.

Their kick was short and wobbly, and nearly blocked by Gino as he tore in hard. The ball was put in play on the City High twenty-two yard line, first and ten, and the goal line was a long way off.

"We can make it," Whip said in the huddle. "Everybody hit."

It seemed to be a different Whip Grogan handling this City High team now. In other games, and in practice sessions Whip had been tough and contemptuous, never too friendly with anyone, but since the previous night and the fight with the Barons, he was a changed boy. Gino could almost see him grow, as he had grown himself.

Whip tried Bruno around the end, but Bruno's running was considerably handicapped this afternoon by the soggy turf. Bruno needed hard, firm ground for those twinkling feet, and he was dragged down before he could get into the open. There was no gain on the play.

In the huddle, Whip was frowning. "This is not the place to pass," he said, "but we're going to."

"Ball's slippery," Johnny pointed out. "If they intercept another one on us, it might be the game, Whip."

"I know it," Whip growled, "but we're going to pass. We'll keep them short and hard. All right, Gino?"

"All right," Gino nodded grimly. "I'll hold them."

"14-P," Whip grinned, and they trotted to their positions.

West Side wasn't looking for passes deep in City territory, and the first one Gino caught easily for a nine-yard gain. Whip threw it hard and low, and the ball plunked against Gino's chest.

Two West Side boys hit him, and he was down, but they had made a nice gain.

"Gino, again," Whip said. "I'll fake it to Lou, first. 10-A."

10-A was a fake hand-off to Lou Winfield, and then Whip faded, and shot the ball out to Gino again as Gino darted over the center. It was another eight-yard gain, and the City High crowd started to cheer a little.

"We'll mix it up," Whip said.

He sent Johnny into the line, and this time Johnny made four yards on a straight buck because the West Side secondaries were watching Gino as he streaked out as if going for another pass.

"We have them on the run," Johnny whispered when he came back. "They're not so sure of themselves."

Whip threw another short pass to Gino, and they made a second first down in succession, the first time they had done that.

Gino held on to the passes like grim death even though there were players all around him, ready to strike him down. He made his catch, and he advanced as far as he could with the ball.

Now Whip alternated by flipping a pass to Bruno, and Bruno made eleven yards on the play, and another first down, and the City High crowd was really beginning to buzz now. It seemed that at last this supposedly strong jayvee squad was finding itself.

They went over the mid-field stripe and started the long march down toward the opposite goal line, and West Side was flustered. Whip's short, sharp passes had them worried. They did not know how to set up a defense against him.

When the backs watched for the passes, Whip sent Johnny or Lou into the line, and now the City High line came alive also and started to dig in.

Benny, Milton Gruber, and Joe Basilo, holding down the middle, charged as one man, opening up the holes. They got down to the West Side twenty-five yard line, and Bruno fumbled as he took a hand-off from Whip.

A West Side boy recovered, and all their labor was in vain. West Side kicked far up the field, and the long journey had to begin over again.

Bruno left the field for a rest, and he was crying again as he trotted toward the bench. Wayne Mc-Carthy met him and put an arm around his shoulders, leading him to the bench.

They went into the fourth quarter with the score still 20-7 for West Side, and time running out.

"Only way we can make it," Whip said, "is with passes. We have to make a lot of yards quick."

Gino knew what that meant. Bruno was out of the game. Charlie Brock, the right end, was a poor receiver, and Mr. McCarthy never had Whip throw to him. Lou Winfield was the other receiver. Either Lou or Gino was to catch those passes.

Whip sent the first one to Lou, using Gino as a decoy. Lou caught it for a six-yard gain, but he didn't get up right away after he'd been tackled. Lou sat on the ground, grimacing in pain, rubbing his right ankle, which he had twisted slightly when the West Side boy had tackled him.

They helped Lou from the field, giving him a big hand, and he was through for the afternoon.

Whip stared at Gino. He said slowly, "All right, Ginzo. You."

"Just throw it," Gino said. "Throw it hard."

"They'll be watching you all the time," Whip told him. "They'll probably have a couple of players guarding you now."

"Just throw it," Gino said.

He went out for the first pass, and he tried to remember the tricks Wayne McCarthy had taught him during the past month. A pass receiver had not only to catch the ball, but he had to get into the clear, away from tacklers, and that meant fast running, shifty running, and feinting.

Mr. McCarthy had taught him how to do that, and this afternoon he ran the way he'd never run before. He ran with his heart and his head and his legs, and he got away from the boys chasing him. When he got away, Whip fired the ball at him.

He caught one for twelve yards; he caught another for nine yards, and then a third for fifteen yards, and City High was screaming for a score. They were down on the West Side eighteen again, and Bruno came back into the game.

But Bruno was still unnerved, and when Whip

threw him a pass into the end zone he dropped it, and they lost the score. A few days before, Whip would have cursed the little Polish boy, but this afternoon he just grinned and said, "We'll get it over."

Johnny plowed down the middle like a miniature bull for eight yards to the ten, and then Whip cleverly faked the hand-off to Bruno, faded, and threw the ball like a shot to Gino in the end zone.

Gino, running like mad, darting in and out, was in the clear for a moment. He reached for the ball, remembering that terrible incident in the Washington game when he dropped a pass in the end zone.

This one he did not drop. He held on to it like grim death as the orange-clad tacklers smothered him, but it was a City High score.

Johnny kicked the point, and it was 20-14 for West Side.

"We'll get 'em," Whip said, and he patted Gino on the back gravely.

Wayne McCarthy watched them from the side lines, and there was a small smile on his face.

"How much time?" Benny asked.

There was less than five minutes remaining, and City had to kick off to West Side which would give them possession of the ball.

Gino lined up on his side of the field as Johnny prepared to kick off.

"Watch for fumbles," Whip yelled across the line.

They went down after Johnny's kick, and the West Side boy caught it and ran upfield to the thirty-seven before little Benny threw him.

It was a new City High jayvee team on the field now, a hard, driving team, unwilling to accept defeat. They charged like one man when West Side put the ball in play, and three tacklers hit the West Side runner behind the line of scrimmage, throwing him for a four-yard loss.

West Side tried to run again, and Gino came in from the rear, circling the line, catching up with the boy, throwing him for a six-yard loss.

Worriedly, West Side called time out, and their coach sent in several substitutes.

"When they kick," Whip said to Gino, "you get in there and block it. You hear?"

"I hear," Gino said.

West Side prepared to kick, and Gino crouched out on the end of the line. He saw Benny striving to move in also; the whole City High line had one thought in mind—to block the West Side kick and take possession of the ball, deep in West Side territory. They were on the West Side twenty-seven yard line with three minutes or less remaining to play.

The West Side kicker drew back, waiting for the ball as the quarterback called his signals. The spin-back was good, exactly the right height, and the kicker trotted forward, dropping the ball toward his right toe.

Gino was in close, fighting his way around a blocker. Out of the corner of his eye, he saw little Benny coming through, reaching for the ball, but the kicker got it away—a long, beautiful kick up the field.

Gino wanted to cry as he tumbled forward, reaching futilely for the ball. Benny lay on his face with him, digging his fingers into the grass.

Bruno, at safety, caught the ball and tried valiantly to get away, but was thrown on the fifty-yard line. The seconds were ticking away rapidly now as they put the ball in play.

"No time to run," Whip scowled. "It's up to you, Gino. 10-P."

Gino went out and cut in, and Whip fired the ball at him. It was good for a twelve-yard gain. He knew that Whip was going to throw to him all the time now because he couldn't trust poor little Bruno, who was a bundle of nerves, and he couldn't depend upon anyone else to catch those hard passes.

"You again, Ginzo," Whip said.

"Throw it," Gino told him.

Whip threw it like a bullet, and Gino caught it for another ten-yard gain, down to the West Side twenty-eight yard line.

The West Side team was all waiting for him now, knowing that Whip had to pass in these few remaining moments, and knowing that the pass would go to Gino, but still they couldn't stop him.

"Run, Gino," Benny whispered. "Run, *Italiano*, like you never ran before."

Gino had been running all afternoon. His legs hurt; his chest hurt; he'd been tackled so many times, and tackled hard. He listened to Whip's signal, and then he lined up, and he ran. He ran like a madman, darting back and forth as Whip faded deeper and deeper with the ball, West Side boys chasing him. Then Whip threw, and Gino leaped, and the ball was against his chest again, and he was on the West Side fourteen.

They were going wild in the City High stands.

"We can't lose," Whip said.

"We can't lose," Gino repeated.

It was another short pass, savagely hard, the ball driving between players, and slamming against Gino's chest. They were on the seven-yard line.

"One more," Benny prayed. "One more, Whip. One more, Gino."

The whole West Side team was waiting for the pass. They knew it was coming, and they spread out. They watched Gino. They watched Whip talk to him, but they didn't hear what Gino said to Whip.

"Give it to Johnny," Gino said. "Let him run. He'll score through the middle."

"It's the last play," Whip wanted to argue. He could have argued that it was Gino's due to score this winning touchdown. He was playing brilliant football this afternoon.

"Let Johnny run," Gino said. "He'll make it. The middle is open, and they're watching me."

"7-A," Whip said.

It was a delayed buck through the middle. Whip was to fade with the ball as if seeking his receiver, and then give the fullback a little lateral toss, and Johnny was to go down the middle with it.

"Open that hole for him," Gino said. "You hear me, Benny?"

"There'll be a hole," Benny whispered.

They lined up again, and the West Side team tensed for the play. Gino pulled out wide, the way he had been doing all along, and they watched him; they worried about him because he had been driving them crazy with his running.

He went out fast, breaking toward the side lines, drawing men with him, running hard, turning, calling for the ball, and it fooled West Side completely.

Benny, Milton Gruber, and Joe Basilo roared through to open the hole. Whip faded with the ball, watching Gino run. Then he tossed that short, soft pass to Johnny, and Johnny let loose.

He went through like a catapult, head lowered, the ball against his chest, heavy legs driving. The hole in the line was there, little Benny struggling forward, panting, gasping, shoving his heavier opponent forward.

Gino saw it all as he held up his hands as if to receive a pass, and he smiled as he saw it. Johnny Anderson kept going, over the five-yard line, yard after yard, down to the goal line, boiling over into the end zone, and with three orange-clad West Side boys clinging to him.

The score was tied at twenty all.

Pandemonium reigned on the field. Gino came back, grinning, and Whip threw his arms around him. The white-faced, breathless Johnny still held the ball against his chest, and the referee had to take it away from him to set it up for the extra point play.

"Can you do it, Johnny?" the City boys asked him.

"I can do it," Johnny Anderson nodded, and he kicked the ball cleanly between the uprights, giving City High a 21-20 victory.

*   *   *   *   *

The sun was no longer shining when they left the field. It was growing dark, and heavy clouds scudded across the face of the sky. Gino walked with Whip and Benny.

As they walked Whip said, "This is the start of

it. We have a couple of years now with the varsity."

"They'll never stop us," Benny said, and Gino looked at him.

"Don't start that again," he warned, and then he threw an arm around Benny's shoulder because Benny was his best friend. Then as they walked, he put another arm around Whip's shoulder. Whip, also, was his friend.